He Couldn't Let His Guard Down And Think Of Her As A Woman.

He had an investigation to run and involvement with Lucy Royall would compromise his objectivity. Compromise him. He was ethically bound to keep emotional distance between them.

"Hayden?" she asked breathlessly.

He gripped the steering wheel until his fingers hurt, trying to anchor himself to something. "Yes?"

"Were you about to kiss me?"

His heart stuttered to a stop. He should have known Lucy wasn't the type of woman to let things lie, to choose the sensible path. "There was a moment, before I thought better of it," he admitted.

"I wish you had."

Dear Reader,

Receiving an invitation to participate in the Daughters of Power: The Capital continuity was fabulous—as a longtime fan of *The West Wing,* writing a book set in D.C. was a delicious opportunity. And the chance to work with five other Harlequin Desire authors made it all the more special.

When I first met Hayden and Lucy, their roles in the overall story were already set, as were some aspects of their personal lives, such as Hayden having a one-year-old son, Josh. So, instead of creating them from scratch, it felt more like being introduced to them, getting to know them—searching out more details of their personalities and lives. I quickly fell in love with the honorable, sexy Hayden, and I came to adore Lucy with her inner strength, as well as her sense of fun.

Though, I have to admit to having a rather large soft spot for Rosebud the bulldog from the moment she ambled onto the page. She took her name from one of my mother's dogs, Roxiana Rosebud, who kept me company during much of the writing of this book. Even though Roxy is a Labrador-rottweiler mix, she's as sweet as Rosebud, so I thought it was fitting she was immortalized by donating her name to Graham's dog.

Finding their happy-ever-after isn't easy for Hayden and Lucy—they have to work for it—but I'm so glad with how their lives turn out. I hope you enjoy Hayden, Lucy, Josh and Rosebud's story!

Cheers,

Rachel

RACHEL BAILEY

NO STRANGER TO SCANDAL

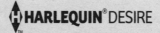
HARLEQUIN® DESIRE

Special thanks and acknowledgment to Rachel Bailey for her contribution to the Daughters of Power miniseries.

Recycling programs
for this product may
not exist in your area.

ISBN-13: 978-0-373-73235-7

NO STRANGER TO SCANDAL

Printed in U.S.A.

www.Harlequin.com

For my father, Colin.

You didn't live to see my name on a book cover,
but I know you'd have been proud. I miss you.

Acknowledgments:

Thanks to Barbara DeLeo and Sharon Archer for reading
early drafts of this book and your insightful comments.
And to Bron and Heather for the cheer squad.

Thanks to the other authors in the Daughters of Power
continuity—it's been a pleasure working with you.
And to Charles Griemsman, the editor for the series—
as always, your guidance was invaluable.

Books by Rachel Bailey

Harlequin Desire

Return of the Secret Heir #2118
What Happens in Charleston... #2138
No Stranger to Scandal #2222

Silhouette Desire

Claiming His Bought Bride #1992
The Blackmailed Bride's Secret Child #1998
At the Billionaire's Beck and Call? #2039
Million-Dollar Amnesia Scandal #2070

Other titles by this author available in ebook format.

RACHEL BAILEY

developed a serious book addiction at a young age (via Peter Rabbit and Jemima Puddleduck) and has never recovered. Just how she likes it. She went on to earn degrees in psychology and social work, but is now living her dream—writing romance for a living.

She lives on a piece of paradise on Australia's Sunshine Coast with her hero and four dogs, where she loves to sit with a dog or two, overlooking the trees and reading books from her evergrowing to-be-read pile.

Rachel would love to hear from you and can be contacted through her website, www.rachelbailey.com.

heavily made up with expertly applied gray smudges and mascara, she looked far too young, too innocent, to be mixed up in the dirty business of ANS illegally hacking into the phones of the president's friends and family. But looks could be deceiving, especially when it came to pampered princesses. No one knew that better than he did.

Lucy Royall had been billionaire Graham Boyle's stepdaughter since she was twelve, and her own deceased father had left her a vast fortune. She hadn't been born with a plain old silver spoon in her mouth—hers had been pure platinum and diamond-encrusted.

He dropped the photo and picked up one of another blonde journalist—ANS senior reporter Angelica Pierce. Only ten minutes ago he'd completed an interview with Ms. Pierce, so he could vouch for both the perfectly white, straight teeth in her plastic broadcast news journalist smile and her aqua eyes. There was something strange about that shade of blue—it looked more like colored contacts than natural. But she spent half her life in front of a TV camera. Angelica Pierce wouldn't be alone in the industry if she was trying to make the most of what she had to look good for the viewers.

Angelica had been eager to help, saying the phone hacking scandal tainted all journalists. And she'd been especially eager to help on the subject of Lucy Royall. Apparently, when Lucy had graduated from college, Boyle had handed her the job of junior reporter over many more qualified applicants, and now, according to Angelica, Lucy could be found "swanning around the office like she's on a movie set, refusing assignments she doesn't like and expecting privileges."

Hayden glanced back at Lucy's photo, with her silk shirt and modest diamond earrings—all tastefully un-

One

Hayden Black flicked through the documents and photos scattered across his D.C. hotel suite desk until he found the one he needed. Hauntingly beautiful hazel eyes; shoulder-length blond hair that shone as if polished; designer-red lips. Lucy Royall. The key to his investigation for Congress that would bring down her stepfather, Graham Boyle.

After his preliminary research from his New York base, he'd decided the twenty-two-year-old heiress who'd been handed life on a silver platter was the weak link he'd target to gather all the information on Graham Boyle's criminal activities. His first appointment this morning had been to get a colleague's take on Ms. Royall so he would be prepped when he met her.

He flicked the photo to the side and picked up another—this one her publicity shot from Boyle's news network, American News Service, where Lucy worked as a junior reporter. Even with the professional tone and her eyes derstated yet subtly conveying wealth and class. He could believe she had a sense of entitlement.

But during the interview, Angelica had done something particularly interesting. She'd lied to him about Lucy threatening her. The signs in her body language had been almost imperceptible, but he'd interviewed countless people over the years and was used to picking up what other people missed.

Of course, there were reasons she might lie—a star reporter watching a young, pretty journalist who happened to be related to the network's owner coming up through the ranks would be nervous. People lied for less every day.

But something told him there was more to the story. Admittedly, his first instinct was always to distrust journalists—they were too used to manipulating facts to make a good story. But this whole investigation centered around journalists, so for objectivity's sake, he'd have to put that aside and take them as they came for now.

He shuffled the photos till he found one of Graham Boyle. Hayden's background research for the congressional committee's investigation into phone hacking and other illegal activities kept leading him back to Boyle.

And his stepdaughter.

Angelica Pierce might have lied about Lucy Royall threatening her, perhaps to protect her job. But he had no trouble believing that Ms. Royall was a spoiled princess playing at being a journalist. Which suited him just fine. Coaxing an admission from her about Boyle's dirty dealings would be a piece of cake—he'd had enough experience with pampered heiresses to know exactly how to handle them.

Lucy Royall was going down, and taking her stepfather with her.

* * *

Lucy wedged the phone between her shoulder and ear and kept typing up the questions for Mitch Davis, the anchor of one of ANS's nightly news shows. He was interviewing a Florida senator in four hours and wanted the list by midday to give himself a chance to familiarize himself with it. Which gave her exactly ten more minutes, and she had an appointment with the congressional committee's criminal investigator, Hayden Black, at one. So the call from Marnie Salloway, one of the news producers, was bad timing. Though that was exactly how this job always seemed to work—too many tasks, too many bosses.

"Marnie, can I call you back in fifteen?"

"I'll be in a meeting then. I need to talk to you now," Marnie snapped.

"Okay, sure." Lucy smiled so her voice sounded pleasant despite her frantic mood. "What do you need?"

"What I need is a list of locations to send the cameraman this afternoon to get the background footage for the story on the president's daughter tonight."

Lucy frowned and kept typing. "I emailed that this morning."

"You sent a list of ten options. Not enough. Have twenty in my inbox by twelve-thirty."

Lucy glanced at the glowing red digital clock on the wall. Nine minutes to twelve. She held back a sigh. "All right, you'll have it."

She replaced the receiver and wasted a precious twenty seconds by dropping her aching head to her desk. When she'd graduated, Graham had offered her a job as a full-fledged reporter. She'd refused, so he'd offered her the spot as a weekend anchor. He was just trying to help her, as he'd done since she was twelve, but she didn't want a top job.

No, that wasn't true—she definitely wanted a top reporting job. But she wanted to earn it, to be *good*. To be respected for her journalistic ability. And the only way to develop that expertise was to work under the great journalists, to learn the skills.

But days like today had her questioning that decision, or at least questioning the decision to take a junior-reporter role at ANS. She wasn't the only junior here, but she was the only one treated like an indentured servant. And the person who'd treated her the worst had been her former hero, Angelica Pierce. Drawing in a deep breath, she went back to typing the last questions for Mitch Davis's interview and emailed them to him with three minutes to spare, then called up the list of locations she'd emailed Marnie for the background footage and opened her web browser to look for alternatives.

It had been made very clear to her on her first day that the other ANS staff resented having Graham's stepdaughter in their newsroom. Rumors had made it back to her that they suspected she was a spy for Graham. Lucy was pretty sure their antagonism was misplaced resentment for authority—people always loved to dig the boot into the boss, and she represented the boss to them. In some ways she couldn't blame them, but she wouldn't let them get to her. Her policy had been to keep her head down and do every menial task the more senior staff asked of her, ridiculous or not.

She sent the extended list to Marnie, grabbed her bag and ran out the door for her meeting with Hayden Black. If she caught a cab and there wasn't too much traffic, she'd make it with a few minutes to spare. On the street, she grabbed a coffee and raspberry muffin, stuffed the muffin in her scarlet hold-all handbag and took a long sip of the coffee before hailing a cab. This was one meeting she didn't want to arrive at late—Congress was wasting time and money on a wild-goose chase, investigating her stepfather for illegal phone-hacking practices at ANS despite already having the culprits in custody. Today was her turn to be interviewed, to defend Graham. He'd been there for whatever she needed for almost half her life; now she would be there for him.

The cab dropped her at the Sterling Hotel, where Hayden Black was staying and conducting his interviews. Apparently he'd been offered an office for his investigation but he preferred neutral territory—an interesting move. Most investigators liked the extra authority afforded by an official office. She sipped the last of her coffee in the elevator and checked her reflection in the mirrored wall— the wind had blown her hair all over the place. The doors slid open as she combed her fingers through the disheveled mess to make it more presentable. First impressions counted, and Graham was depending on her.

She checked the number on the hotel suite door, then knocked with the hand holding the empty paper cup, straightening her skirt with her other. She looked around for a trash can, but turned back when she heard the door open and started to smile in an I've-got-nothing-to-hide way.

And froze, the smile only half-formed.

A tall man in a crisp white shirt, crimson tie and neatly pressed dark trousers filled the doorway—Hayden Black. The air shifted around her, became heavier, uneven. She'd met a lot of powerful men in her job, in her life, yet none had had the *presence* of this man before her, as if his energy somehow flowed out and charged the space around him. The thicker air was difficult to draw into her lungs and she had to struggle to fill them.

Frown lines formed across his forehead. Dark brown

eyes stared at her from a lightly weathered face, and they didn't seem to like what they saw. Her skin cooled. He was judging her already and the interview hadn't even begun. All her resilience coalesced, snapping her out of whatever flight of fancy had overtaken her for those moments, and she straightened her spine. That was more than fine—she was used to people judging her based on preconceived ideas about her wealth, her lifestyle and her upbringing. An investigator for Congress was just one more to add to the list. She lifted her chin and waited.

He cleared his throat. "Ms. Royall. Thank you for coming."

"My pleasure, Mr. Black," she said using the polite voice her mother had taught her to always start with when she wanted to win something. *You catch more flies with honey than vinegar, Lucy.*

He extended an arm to show her through the door. "Can I get you anything before we start?" His voice was gruff, unwelcoming.

"I'm fine, thank you." She took a seat and put the holdall bag on the floor beside her.

He lowered himself into the chair opposite and granted her a condescending glance. "We'll run through some simple questions about ANS and your stepfather. If you keep your answers to the truth, we shouldn't experience any trouble."

A surge of heat rushed across her skin. The patronizing jerk. If she kept her answers to the truth, they shouldn't experience any trouble? She was twenty-two, had a degree from Georgetown University and owned one-sixth of the biggest department-store chain in the country. Did he think she would accept being treated like a child?

She gave him her best guileless smile, reached for her large red bag and deposited it on the desk in front of her.

Then she combined the sweet voice of her mother with the rapid-fire manner she'd learned from Graham, laying on her North Carolina accent extra thick for good measure. "You know, I think I will have a glass of water, if that's okay. I've got a muffin here I'd like to eat—you don't mind, do you?—I skipped lunch to make this meeting and I'll think more clearly with some food in my stomach."

He hesitated, then murmured, "Of course," and rose to get her water.

She took a satisfied breath—she'd thrown him off balance. When he put the glass in front of her, she handed him her paper coffee cup. "And could you throw this away for me while you're up? I didn't want to put it in my bag in case any residual moisture leaked out, and there wasn't a trash can in the hallway." He took the cup, but seemed far from happy about it. She smiled at him again. "Thank you. You'd be surprised how many people refuse a simple request, but then again, you're a criminal investigator. Maybe you wouldn't." She broke off a piece of muffin and popped it into her mouth.

He sat back in his chair and stared at her, hard. Seemed he'd regained his balance. "Ms. Royall—"

Swallowing, she reached into her bag and came out with a notepad. "I'm going to take notes on what we talk about. I always find it's best if everyone remembers exactly what's said in interviews, whatever kind they are. Helps everyone keep their answers to the truth and that way we shouldn't run into trouble." She broke off another piece of her muffin and held it out to him. "Raspberry muffin?"

His eyes narrowed and she wondered if she'd pushed too far. But he simply said, "No." Albeit with a stern finality.

"It's a very good muffin." She slipped the piece into her mouth and reached into her bag again for a pen.

"Are you ready?" he asked in a tight voice.

She looked down at her pen and clicked it. "Just give me one more moment. I'd rather be fully prepared for an important conversation like this." She put her bag on the floor again, and wrote at the top of her page,

Hayden Black interview. April 2, 2013.

Then she beamed up at him. "I'm ready."

Hayden resisted the impulse to groan and instead called up the neutral expression that was normally easy to find in an interview. Lucy Royall was exactly like her photo, yet nothing like it. Her hair was shiny and blond, but sitting haphazardly around her shoulders, as if she'd stood in a gust of D.C. wind. Her lips were the same as the photo, but were bronze today, and full, sensual, as they moved while she ate the muffin. Despite his intentions, his breath hitched. Her eyes were the same shade of hazel, but in person they shone with intelligence. He knew she was trying to play him, and damned if she wasn't having some success. And he was unsure if that irritated or amused him.

But one thing that didn't amuse him was his unexpected reaction when he'd first opened the door. He'd been thunderstruck. She wasn't merely beautiful, she was breathtaking. There was a light around her, inside her. A glow that was so appealing, he'd had to focus hard so his hand wouldn't reach out. And was there a more inappropriate woman on the planet for him to have a reaction this strong to? The daughter of the man he was investigating on behalf of a congressional committee. A woman who, if his guess was correct, was complicit in her stepfather's illegal activities.

The woman herself raised her brows, either because

his face had contorted with self-disgust or because she was sitting there, pen poised, waiting for him to start the interview while he merely stared.

Clearing his throat, he thumbed the button to start the recording equipment. "Tell me about your relationship with Graham Boyle."

She didn't hesitate. "Graham has been my stepfather since I was twelve years old. He's a sweet man with a good heart."

Sweet? In another setting he may have laughed. The man owned a national cable-news network and was feared by competitors and allies alike. For Graham Boyle, the ends justified the means—he demanded that his reporters do anything to get a story.

And someone who'd been part of Graham Boyle's immediate family for ten years couldn't be completely unaware of his ruthless nature.

"That's not the common perception," he said mildly.

"Do your parents see you the same way your friends do, Mr. Black? Your girlfriends? Employees? Bosses?" She drew in a breath and seemed to grow taller in her seat. "My stepfather has the type of job where he has to make tough decisions, and people who disagree with those decisions might see him as hard-hearted. But he has been nothing but kind and generous to me."

"I'm glad to hear it. But he hasn't been accused of making tough decisions, Ms. Royall. He's been accused of authorizing or at least condoning illegal phone hacking to obtain information about the president's illegitimate daughter."

She stilled. The only movement was the rapid rise and fall of her chest. Then she leaned forward, slowly, deliberately. "Let me tell you what sort of man he is. When my mother died three years ago, Graham was devastated. He could barely walk away from the graveside service—he had to be supported by two family friends, he was that riddled with grief. Then, despite the hours his job demands, and his own grief, he made a point of calling me, visiting, bringing me gifts. Making sure I was okay." She sat back again, but her body remained tense. "He's a good man."

There was something deeply attractive about her impassioned defense of her stepfather. The way her eyes sparked made his breath catch. Made his pulse that much faster—a far from ideal response to an interviewee. Determinedly, he ignored it. He was a professional.

"Al Capone was good to his family," he said.

Her cheeks flushed red. "I resent the heck out of your implication."

He flicked his pen between the fingers of his right hand and arched a brow. "I wasn't implying anything beyond pointing out that being good to his family doesn't automatically exclude a person from engaging in illegal activities."

Lucy held his gaze across the table for long, challenging seconds. He let the silence lengthen. In situations like this, patience was his friend.

She dropped her gaze to the pad of paper in front of her and her blond hair swung forward a little. An image rose in his mind of threading his fingers through her hair, of tilting her face up to him, of lowering his own until his mouth gently touched hers, of feeling the softness of her plump lips, the passion she—

Suddenly his shirt collar was too tight. Damn it, what was he doing? In an important investigation like this, he couldn't afford to be attracted to a witness.

Get ahold of yourself, Black.

He drew in a breath and stared at her until all he saw was a woman covering up for a criminal.

"Have you participated in any instances of illegal surveillance at ANS?" he asked, more harshly than he'd intended.

"No," she said, lacing her fingers together on the table in front of her.

Without missing a beat, he continued. "Are you aware of any instances of illegal surveillance at ANS?"

"No, I'm not." Her voice was measured, even.

"Have you participated in or been aware of any instances of any illegal activity at ANS?"

"No."

"Did you work with former ANS journalists Brandon Ames and Troy Hall when they used illegal phone hacking to uncover the story about the president's illegitimate daughter?"

"No."

"Were they carrying out orders from your stepfather?"

"Of course not."

"They initially blamed the phone hacking on a temporary researcher, but the researcher was clean. Do you know who it was at ANS who helped them?"

"As far as I know, no one."

"What's your take on why the accusations have been made against ANS and Graham Boyle?"

She let out a long breath. "Those who make something of their lives always attract those who want to tear them down."

Unfortunately, he knew that wasn't where the accusations had originated. Graham Boyle might have a good point or two, might treat his stepdaughter well, but he was still a ruthless jerk who'd hurt many.

"How do you think ANS came up with the leads that uncovered President Morrow's daughter? He was a Montana senator before his presidential campaign—it's not as if no one's looked into his background before."

For the first time, an uncertain line appeared between her brows. "I don't know. I wasn't working on that story."

He knew he had to push further, but God help him, with that look on her face, he wanted to reassure her instead. To take her hand across the table and tell her everything would be okay. Despite that, the cynical part of his brain knew it was probably an act. He needed to listen to that side of himself more.

"But you talk to other journalists, surely," he said, thankfully hitting the skeptical note he'd aimed for. "And this story and its methods are very high profile. You're telling me you've heard nothing about how they got the lead?"

"Good old investigative journalism—it's hard to beat." Her perkiness was forced, but he didn't get the sense she was lying in an underhanded way. Not like the last woman who'd sat in that chair. This was a woman who didn't get on with her colleagues, felt excluded from them and was covering up for that. A shaft of unwanted tenderness hit him squarely in the chest.

But Angelica Pierce had made it clear whose fault that lack of integration was. Feeling sorry for Lucy Royall was a dangerous trap. He rubbed a hand over his face. This interview wasn't working, wasn't getting him anywhere. Perhaps the lack of sleep over the past few months was finally affecting his investigative edge.

Hayden glanced at his watch. Maybe it'd be better to finish early today, pick up his son from the nanny next door and go for a walk in one of D.C.'s parks. He could interview Lucy Royall again when his focus was stronger.

"Thanks for your time," he said, his voice almost a growl. "I'll be in touch when I need to speak with you again."

She tucked her notebook and pen into her bag and

stood. "Mr. Black, I understand that you're just doing your job. But I hope you haven't already discounted the possibility that Graham Boyle might be innocent."

Hayden pushed to his feet and rested his hands low on his hips. "If the evidence shows he's innocent, Ms. Royall, that's what I'll report back to Congress."

But his gut instinct never lead him astray, and his gut told him that Lucy Royall's stepfather was as guilty as they came. It was up to him to prove it.

He held the door open for her then watched her walk down the hall, her hips subtly swaying. Beauty and a glorious accent had covered surprising strength and determination in his interviewee—and had caught him off guard.

Luckily, he was even more determined.

Next time he met Lucy Royall, he'd be ready for her.

Two

Lucy quietly slipped through the door to her stepfather's office—his secretary had told her he was on the phone but to go through anyway. Graham nodded when he saw her, then barked more orders at whoever was on the other end of the line.

Used to being in the background while he worked, Lucy took the chance to look through his top-floor window at the panoramic view of D.C. She loved this city. She'd moved here from Charlotte, North Carolina, when she was twelve and her mother had married Graham. The town—and Graham—had been good to her.

From a basket under the desk, Rosebud, his bulldog, lifted her head and, recognizing Lucy, lumbered out to greet her. Lucy dropped her bag beside the chair and crouched down to rub the dog's velvety, wrinkled face.

"How's it going, Rosie?" she whispered and was rewarded with a wide doggie smile, complete with a pink tongue almost curled back on itself.

With a final terse comment, Graham ended the call and crossed the room.

"Lucy!" he boomed and held out his arms. She stood and leaned into his bear hug, letting go of all her worries for a few precious seconds. He was the one person she could always count on. Her only family.

"Hang on," he said, pulling back. "I've got something here for you."

She couldn't help the smile at the familiar words. "You didn't have to."

"Of course I did." And she knew he was right—it was the way he showed love. In the same way he was her only family, she was all Graham had. They made an odd couple in some ways, but their unusual little family worked for them.

He opened a door in the sleek cabinets that lined one wall and pulled out a deep blue velvet box. He handed it to her, his grin proud. She opened the lid and took out an exquisite crystal bulldog the size of her palm.

"It's Rosebud." At the sound of her name, the real Rosebud thumped her curly tail on the carpet. "Thank you," Lucy said and kissed Graham's cheek.

Graham smiled with his heart in his eyes, as he always did in these moments, then he cleared his throat and strode back to his desk. He'd never been particularly comfortable with emotions, so the moments, although heartfelt, were always short. "Tell me how the interview with Black went."

She sank into an upholstered armchair in front of Graham's heavy desk. "Shorter than I expected." She'd puzzled over that on the cab ride back. "He only asked a few questions, really."

He flicked his wrist dismissively. "That means he was just taking your temperature. There will be more."

"He said he'd be in touch when he needed to speak to me again." Remembering Hayden's words—and his deep voice saying them—sent a shiver across her skin. If she wasn't careful, she'd develop a crush on the investigator, which would be bad on more levels than she could count. But, oh, that man had been delicious. So tall and broad, with a dark, brooding demeanor to accompany his looks. Even his hands had fascinated her—he'd flicked his pen over and under his fingers as he'd considered a point and she'd been mesmerized. They were long fingers with blunt ends, dexterous, lightly tanned. Instead of paying attention to the questions, for one sublime, stolen moment she had imagined his palm cupping the side of her face, those fingers stroking her cheek.

Graham leaned back in his chair and laced his own fingers behind his head, bringing her attention back to the present. And to the gravity of the issue on the table.

"Our biggest risk here," he said, eyes narrowed and aimed at a point on the wall, "is that someone with an ax to grind will falsify testimony. Feed Black lies and say they saw something." He glanced back to her. "Did you get a sense from him that he's got anything like that?"

"He played his cards close to his chest. But one thing was obvious," she said gently, as if she could soften the blow. "He thinks you're guilty."

Graham swore under his breath. "I refuse to sit back and wait for an investigator who's not objective to 'find' evidence to support his theory. We need to expose Black before he does too much damage."

She tilted her head to the side. "What do you have in mind?"

"I want you to start your own investigation," he said in his trademark firecracker rhythm. "I'm taking you off all other duties. You'll run this on your own. No word to anyone else. You're the only one I can trust one hundred percent not to stab me in the back for the notoriety, or whatever-the-hell reason people frame other people for."

None of it was a question, but he was waiting for her response. She reached over and clasped one of his cold hands between hers. "I'll start right away."

"You're a good girl." He patted her hands, then released them. "Congress will have vetted him for the job, dug into his past, but we're better. Find the skeletons in his closet and bring them out to play. We'll air an exposé as soon as you have enough."

Her insides fluttered. This wasn't a style of journalism that she liked or particularly wanted to be involved in. And Hayden Black being the target made her even less comfortable. She shifted in her chair. The discomfort could have been a result of the stirrings of attraction, but she still didn't like the idea of targeting him.

Then she remembered his closed-off expression when she'd left his suite less than an hour ago—he was going after Graham, already convinced of his guilt. Doing an exposé might leave a bad taste in her mouth, but Hayden Black's own actions made it necessary. Besides, if he had no skeletons hidden away, there'd be nothing to find.

She nodded, decision made. "You can't have me on air with this. Everyone knows I'm your stepdaughter. We'll need someone with a good reputation and a bit more distance from you."

"We'll worry about that when we have the content ready to go. You do the research, get the story, and I'll bring someone in to host then."

Her mind clicked over into journalist mode and she took out a notebook from her hold-all bag. "Who's our source at the Sterling Hotel?"

Graham picked up the phone on his desk, dialed,

barked an order, then after he had his information, disconnected and looked at Lucy again. "Concierge named Jerry Freethy."

"Okay." She dropped the notebook back in her bag and stood. "I'll keep you up to date." She blew Rosebud an air kiss and headed for the door.

"Lucy," Graham said gruffly, and she turned. "Thank you."

Emotion clogged her throat but she found her voice. "Don't worry about it. I've got your back, Graham."

The next day, at half past one, Lucy saw her target. The concierge had told her Hayden Black liked to take a walk in the park across from the Sterling Hotel with his son on his lunch break, but that the time of the break varied. So Lucy and Rosebud had been wandering the park since just after eleven. Rosebud was panting from the exertion, but thoroughly enjoying her day out meeting random people who stopped to pat her.

Hayden was striding along a paved path about twenty feet away, talking to an infant he carried in one arm, holding a brown paper bag in the other. The sight of him trapped her breath in her lungs. Wide, strong shoulders that tapered to narrow hips. Long legs that walked with confidence and purpose. The masculine grace in the way he held his son.

She swallowed hard. "Come on, Rosie, I have a little boy I want you to meet." Rosebud looked up, her curled tongue poking out as she smiled.

Lucy had spent the afternoon and evening before gathering as much information as she could on Hayden Black. There wasn't a whole lot available on the web, but then, he was a professional investigator, so it made sense that he protected his own information. She'd found New York newspaper articles about his wife's death a few months earlier in a car crash, leaving Hayden the single father of a nine-month-old baby, Joshua, who would now be one year old. And currently wearing denim overalls, a bright-blue hat and a cheeky grin.

As they came closer, Lucy gazed at the trees, their branches heavy with spring flowers, but kept man and child in her peripheral vision. Hayden had his head bent, talking to his son, not paying a lot of attention to where they were, the people rollerblading past or the joggers making their way along the wide path. The hitch in her lungs had smoothed out and now her breaths were coming a little too fast for comfort, which she told herself was excitement about the story, but she suspected had more to do with seeing Hayden Black again.

When they were only ten feet apart, she heard a squeal, followed by, "Goggie!" Lucy finally glanced up to see Hayden had stopped midstep, and probably midsentence, given the way his mouth was open, as if forming a word he'd since forgotten.

She'd never paid much attention to men's mouths—shoulders and biceps had usually caught her attention first—but Hayden's mouth was a thing of beauty. Sensual lips that she could almost feel tracing a path along the side of her neck. Her skin heated and prickled.

Before becoming too carried away, she found a smile and walked Rosie over. A gentle breeze blew her hair around her face, and she tucked it behind her ears as she stopped in front of father and son.

"Ms. Royall," he said. His voice was pleasant, probably for his son's benefit, but his face told a different story—eyebrows slashed down, jaw tight. He was annoyed at running into her. Just because he didn't want to mix work and family? Or was there something more…?

"Lovely day, isn't it?" she said, leaning down to give Rosie a scratch behind the ears. "Little birds in the trees, the flowers are out, the weather's warm—everything is just so perfect. Rosebud and I love April."

A speculative gleam appeared in Hayden's eye. He'd know everything there was to know about Graham from his shoe size to what he liked for breakfast, so knowing Rosie belonged to one of the targets of his investigation was guaranteed. And he'd just realized he could use Rosie to engage Lucy in conversation about Graham, and hope the casual setting caused her to slip up. Precisely what she was doing to him.

Although that didn't explain why he'd been annoyed when he first saw her—he was renowned for his investigative acumen, so that should have been the first thing that occurred to him. Perhaps he hadn't wanted his time with his son to be interrupted. Entirely possible, but it had felt like more than that....

Perhaps he disliked her personally and was annoyed at running into her away from work? Her belly hollowed out before she gave herself a mental shake. Just because her hormones went haywire when she saw him didn't mean the chemistry was mutual. Besides, the man had lost his wife only a few months ago.

She should be pleased that at least one of them wouldn't be carried away by flights of fancy. Getting involved with the man she was investigating, and worse, who was investigating ANS for Congress, would be unthinkable.

"Goggie!" Josh squealed again, apparently impatient to be getting to the dog-patting action.

Hayden looked from Rosie to her. "Is it okay for Josh to pet her?"

"Sure," she said, laying on her Southern accent thick and smiling innocently. "She's as gentle as a lamb."

Hayden crouched down beside her and supported Josh as he found his feet and reached out to touch Rosie's ear.

"Her name's Rosebud," Lucy said to the toddler.

As they watched Josh and Rosie interact, Hayden asked, "How long have you had her?"

"She's Graham's dog," she replied, as if she hadn't worked out that he'd know that. "He's had her for six years. Since she was a puppy."

Hayden leaned forward and joined Josh in petting her. "Nice dog."

His shoulder was only a couple of inches from hers—if she moved a little she'd bump against him. A mischievous impulse urged her to lean into him, knowing he'd be solid and warm, and it took all her willpower to resist. The scent of clean, masculine skin surrounded her, made everything else fade into the background, made a hum resound through her bloodstream.

Rosie rolled over onto her back, producing her tummy for rubs with no shame at her brazen request for attention. Lucy blinked down at the dog, fully aware she walked a knife's edge of being just as obvious. She squared her shoulders. Time to move away from temptation and remember she was a journalist working on a story.

Hayden rubbed the dog, barely able to concentrate on anything but Lucy at his side. Within touching distance. If he wanted to, he could reach out a hand and trail it down her arm. Or wrap his fingers under her curtain of silky blond hair and discover if the skin on her neck was as soft as it appeared. His heart thudded like a bass drum. The jolt of attraction when he'd first seen her in the park had thrown him off balance and part of him was still scrambling to find his equilibrium.

Lucy stood, breaking the spell. "I was just about to give

Rosebud a drink." She took out a bottle of water and a rolled-up waterproof canvas bowl from her bag. "Would Josh like to help?"

Hayden looked down at his son and, for the briefest of moments, was at a loss, uncertain what Josh would or wouldn't like. His gut twisted tight. He hated not instinctively knowing these things. Then he gave himself a mental shake. Of course Josh would like to help — it was a dog and water, both of which spelled fun.

"He'd love to," he finally said.

Lucy gave Josh the bottle of water and explained how to fill the canvas bowl in terms a one-year-old could understand. Josh sloshed more water on the ground and on Lucy than in the bowl, but no one seemed to mind, and soon the dog was enthusiastically drinking and Josh was trying to catch her wagging, curly tail. Hayden's heart expanded to see his son smiling and so obviously filled with joy.

Lucy screwed the top back on the water and slid it into the same large red bag she'd had yesterday at the interview. Seemed she had all contingencies covered inside that bag—yesterday a muffin, notebook and pen; today a water bottle and a dog bowl. He wouldn't be surprised if she pulled out a picnic blanket and folding chairs next.

He sat back on his haunches. "I read somewhere that Graham had a dog that he takes to work each day," he said conversationally.

"This is her." She didn't look up, but gave Rosebud an extra rub on the neck.

"So you spend a bit of time in Graham's office to see Rosebud?"

She smiled, obviously aware of where his questions were leading. The dog finished her drink and Josh, looking for the next interesting adventure, held his arms out to Lucy. Without hesitation, she bundled him in.

"How's it going, Josh?" she said, charming his son, then looked at Hayden over his son's head and said, "I see Graham and Rosie a few times a week."

Instead of following the line of questioning he'd planned in his head, Hayden couldn't draw his eyes from the easy way Lucy interacted with his little boy. Josh had only just met her, but was already happy in her arms. And Lucy was relaxed, as if she knew just what to do with a toddler. Lord above, Hayden wished *he* knew what to do with one. Sure, he had the basics covered, like sleeping, bathing and feeding, but he was still getting used to being the primary caregiver to a child, and most of the time he felt he was swimming out of his depth.

Why did it seem so natural for her? From his research, he knew she had no siblings, no young cousins around, yet she seemed supremely confident where he often felt awkward and unsure. Maybe because he wanted to be a good father so damn much and Lucy had nothing riding on it at all.

He blew out a slow breath and stood—he was losing his focus with Lucy Royall again. This time he'd almost recovered from the force of her allure and managed to steer the conversation toward Graham Boyle, but now he'd become distracted again by her natural way with his son. He rubbed his fingers over his eyes and refocused on his new plan—build rapport and see what else he could discover in the casual setting.

"We're walking this way, how about you?" he said, sinking a hand into his pocket. "Josh and I have just come out for our lunch break."

Lucy beamed over at him. "We'd love to join you for a walk, wouldn't we, Rosie?"

Hayden hoisted Josh up onto his shoulder, but the boy leaned toward Lucy with his arms out. Hayden arched an eyebrow. Josh didn't normally go to new people this easily—why did he have to overcome his trust issues with someone Hayden was investigating?

Lucy laughed and held up Rosebud's lead. "How about we swap?"

Still, he didn't move. Building rapport while taking a walk was one thing, but letting her carry his son, crossing personal lines, was dangerous, and something he'd never done before.

"Daddy," Josh said, pointing to Lucy. "Up."

And right there was his Achilles' heel. Josh wanted Lucy, and Hayden wanted Josh to be happy. Complex ethical issues boiled down to pure simplicity.

"Sure," he said. He took the dog's lead and handed over his son, trying to minimize touching Lucy in both tasks since he was in enough trouble as it was. "I'll take that bag while you have Josh."

"It's fine." She tickled Josh's side and was rewarded with giggles. "I'm used to having it over my shoulder."

He nodded and they started along the paved path that wound alongside the sparkling river, Hayden busy trying not to physically smack himself over the head. He'd been brought in by a congressional committee to investigate ANS, and Graham Boyle in particular. And now here he was, in a D.C. park, talking a stroll with the man's stepdaughter, allowing her to cuddle his son, offering to carry her bag and walking the wretched man's dog.

Not to mention that his pulse was pounding too hard for a casual walk, which had less to do with the exercise than with the woman whose elbow was mere inches from his own. So close he could practically feel all her vibrant energy radiating out and filling the air around her.

He cleared his throat. "Ms. Royall—"

"Lucy." With his son's fist wrapped around her fingers, she glanced up at him. "We're walking in a park on a lunch break. I think you can call me Lucy."

"Lucy, then." The name felt unusual as his mouth moved around the word. He'd only said it aloud together with her surname before, but alone it seemed special, prettier. More intimate.

"Yes?"

He looked down at her, frowning. "Yes, what?"

"You were about to say something when I told you to call me Lucy."

Good point. But he had no idea what it had been. He thrust the fingers of his free hand into his hair. He'd called their interview to a halt because he was getting distracted. Seemed the extra twenty-four hours to regroup hadn't helped any.

He searched his brain for a way to informally find a path to the information he wanted. "Did you always want to be a journalist?"

They waited while Rosebud sniffed the base of a tree, and Lucy shrugged one shoulder. "Maybe not always. But since I interned with Graham when I was sixteen."

"What did you want to be before that?"

"My father's family is in department stores," she said casually. "When he died I inherited his stock. I always thought I'd do a business degree and work there."

Her family was "in department stores"? He almost laughed. In his preliminary research he'd found that Lucy was one of the Royall Department Stores Royalls. A family of old money that stood alongside the Rockefellers, Vanderbilts and Gettys in stature. The woman had pedigree coming out her ears.

Genuine curiosity nibbled. "Have you stayed in touch with that side of your family?"

"Occasionally I see Aunt Judith and her family," she

said softly, with just a tinge of regret. "She has a gorgeous lodge in Fields, Montana, where we sometimes gather for birthdays and Christmases."

"Fields is a nice place," he said. Great ski fields and snowboarding, although now just as famous for being the birthplace of President Morrow as its natural charms.

"We've had some good family times there. Plus, a couple of times a year I go to a board meeting, and occasionally talk to them about charity events."

As she tapped a finger on his son's nose, Hayden watched her and tried to get it all to make sense. Her choices didn't quite add up with the image he had of a pampered princess.

"Wouldn't it have been an easier path to work in the Royall family business? You already own significant stock there. You wouldn't have had to start out at the bottom like you did at ANS." That was what his wife, Brooke, had done—worked in her family's banking empire. But in effect, it had only been role-playing. She'd had a big corner office and taken a lot of long lunches.

Lucy arched a challenging eyebrow. "What makes you think I'd want to take the easier path?"

"Human nature." He didn't try to hide the cynicism in his voice. "Who wouldn't want the easier option?"

She was silent and the moment stretched out; the only sound was Josh's gurgling baby talk. Then she looked up at him with eyes that seemed far too insightful. "Tell me, Hayden, did you take the easiest career option available to you?"

"No," he admitted. But then, he hadn't been brought up an heiress like Lucy or Brooke. Completely different situation.

"How long have you been a criminal investigator?" she asked.

"A few years now." But he wasn't here to talk about himself. He rolled his shoulders back and changed the conversation's direction. "What story are you working on now?"

She moved Josh onto her other hip and adjusted his blue hat. "Are you officially asking me?"

He could sense her reluctance, but that wasn't unusual with journalists trying to keep their scoop under wraps. And since his investigation was about past practices, her current story was irrelevant. He shrugged. "No, just conversation."

"Then I'll pass on the question." She looked up at him and unleashed a dazzling smile. "Did you come out just to walk, or do you have lunch in that bag?"

He held up the brown paper bag. "Lunch. I can offer you half a room-service cheese and tomato on rye." He'd found that when dealing with hotels, the plainer the order, the less likely they were to ruin it with some embellishment meant to impress but usually falling short. He was a man of simple tastes—he'd take sandwiches on fresh bread from the deli near his office over a fancy restaurant lunch any day.

"You can keep your sandwich," she said. "I have mine in my bag."

"Tell me you don't have a picnic blanket in that bag," he said, one corner of his mouth turning up.

Her forehead crinkled into a confused frown. "A picnic blanket wouldn't fit in here."

"You seem to pull out all sorts of things, so a blanket wouldn't have surprised me," he said dryly.

They found a patch of grass under a weeping willow a little farther back from the path. He pulled out a sealed plastic bag with a wet washcloth inside and wiped off Josh's hands before passing him a banana.

"That's pretty organized," Lucy said, watching him with those huge hazel eyes.

His hackles went up. "For a dad, you mean?"

"For anyone." Her head tipped to the side, as if puzzling him out. "I didn't mean it as an insult."

He nodded. Just because he was prickly about his parenting skills didn't mean she'd taken a swipe at him. He offered a self-deprecating smile as compensation for his overreaction. "The nanny packed it all. I wouldn't have thought of a washcloth, so you weren't far off the mark."

She broke off a piece of her granola bar and popped it in her mouth. They ate in silence for a couple of minutes, watching Josh with his banana.

Lucy leaned back, propping one hand on the grass behind her for support. "Is that where Josh is during your interviews?"

"I hired the nanny for while we're in D.C. She comes nine to five." He hadn't been sure how the arrangement would work out, but it was fine. The biggest adjustment had been not having his sister close by—he was flying solo as a parent for the first time, and he was determined to make it work.

"What does Josh normally do during the day?" she asked as she fed a piece of granola to Rosebud.

"When we're in New York, a couple of days a week he goes to my sister—she has a three-year-old boy, and the cousins enjoy their time together. The other three days a week he goes to a day-care center at my office. There are five kids of staff members there, and I can see him at lunchtime."

She smiled over at Josh. "Sounds ideal."

No, ideal would have been Josh having two parents to spend time with him, love him and make him the center of their world. But even before Brooke's death, Josh hadn't had that. The weight of needing to make things perfect for his son crashed down on him, as it did regularly. His gut contracted and clenched. He was all Josh had and he'd do his damned best to make his childhood as close to ideal as he could.

He looked up and saw Lucy was still watching him. This had become far too personal. What was it about Lucy Royall that made him forget everything that was important? What he needed to do was schedule another interview, and this time he'd write a complete list of questions—something he hadn't done in years—to make sure he stayed on topic.

He grabbed the remnants of his lunch and stuffed them back into the brown paper bag. "Josh is getting sleepy. I need to get him back for his nap."

"This was nice," she said, picking up the washcloth and wiping the banana from Josh's fingers. "Maybe Rosie and I could join you again sometime."

Join him again sometime? He coughed out an incredulous laugh. Out in the forest, this was a woman who'd poke a hungry bear until it ate her. He stood and picked Josh up. Thankfully, the little boy curled into his neck, as if supporting Hayden's prediction that he was ready for a nap.

"Look, Lucy," he said, more gruffly than he intended. "I'm not sure what you think is going on here, but this investigation is serious. I'm not here to make friends." Her eyes widened and he immediately regretted his tone. He blew out a breath, and said more softly, "Even if I wanted to, I can't."

Lucy stood, as well. "You'd like to be my friend, Hayden?" She arched an eyebrow, her eyes glimmering with something he couldn't read.

"Under *different circumstances,*" he emphasized, "it's possible that we would have been friends."

Her chin lifted. "I know how important this is. I take Graham's future very seriously. But just so we're clear—" she fixed him with sultry hazel eyes, and her voice slid deeper into the accent of a Southern belle who took no prisoners "—under different circumstances, I wouldn't want to be your friend, Hayden. I'd make one heck of a pass at you."

She turned and walked off, blond hair glinting in the sunshine, Rosie at her heels, leaving Hayden poleaxed.

Three

At four o'clock the next day, Lucy knocked on the door to Hayden's suite, then rolled her shoulders one at a time to try and ease the bunching tension in them.

Hayden had called her cell an hour ago and asked if she could come by to answer a few more questions, and she'd jumped at the chance to see him again in his suite, maybe find a few more clues for her story. The only other time she'd been to his hotel was before Graham had handed her the assignment of the exposé, so this time she'd pay more attention to the little things. The clues.

But now that she was here, her knees quivered—in fact her whole body was unsteady. She wiped damp palms down her calf-length skirt. This was the first time she'd seen him after saying that if things were different, she'd make a pass at him. And she had no idea how things had changed between them, or if she'd ruined the fragile rapport she'd been building with the man who was her target.

After she'd turned a corner yesterday at the park and was safely out of his line of sight, she'd called herself every type of crazy. Rosie had looked up, worried, and Lucy had explained to the dog that she'd probably just uttered the most reckless, foolish words of her life.

Even if they were true.

But she had to be careful. It wasn't just that they were in the midst of a congressional investigation. Hayden Black was the last man on the planet she could afford to be involved with. People already judged her for being the daughter of Jonathon Royall and the stepdaughter of Graham Boyle—two wealthy, high-profile, well-connected men. The common opinion was that she'd been handed everything she wanted on a silver platter. That she hadn't had to work for her own achievements. If she were to be seen with another wealthy, high-profile, well-connected man like Hayden Black, especially given that he was a few years older than she, people would write her off as a woman who was dependent on strong men. Her achievements would again be discounted as not coming from hard work. At just thirteen she'd realized what people assumed about her and it had made her determined to prove to the world that she could achieve anything she wanted on her own.

No, Hayden Black was not for her. She needed an average guy, maybe one just starting out in his career, like her.

With a heavy whoosh, the door swung open and there stood the far-from-average man himself, as broodingly gorgeous as she remembered. "Thank you for coming," he said, his voice like gravel, as if he hadn't used it all day.

And there was something new in his expression—his dark coffee eyes were wary as they assessed her. Seemed she'd thrown the great criminal investigator a curveball yesterday. Her taut shoulders relaxed a little. Perhaps, despite it being a crazy thing to say, it had worked in her favor.

"You're welcome...." She paused as she stepped into the room. "Do I call you Hayden or Mr. Black, since this is an official interview?"

"Hayden is fine." He closed the door behind her and led her to the desk and chairs where they'd spoken two days ago.

She glanced around, taking note of details that might be useful later. Besides the papers on the wooden desk and the coffee cup on the kitchenette counter, the room was neat, nothing out of place, as if he'd just moved in. Hotel housekeeping would have had something to do with that, but there was more to it—as if he was keeping a firm line between Hayden the father and widower and Hayden the tough, take-no-prisoners investigator. She also spied the recorder sitting on the desk again and approved. Recordings were less likely to be misinterpreted than notes.

"Would you like a drink?" he asked.

She took her seat and lifted her bag onto the desk. "I'm fine."

"You're sure?" he asked with a raised eyebrow, and she remembered that last time she'd made him go back for water after they'd sat down, then to throw away her paper coffee cup. Her mouth began to curve at the memory, but as their gazes held, heat shimmered between them. Time seemed to stretch; goose bumps erupted across her skin. Then Hayden looked away and gave his head a quick shake.

"I have a bottle of water in my bag," she said in a voice that was more of a husky whisper.

He folded himself into his chair, as if nothing had just passed between them, and muttered something that sounded suspiciously like, "Of course you do."

She took out her water, notepad and pen and lined them up beside each other, using the extra moments to find her equilibrium.

"Let me know when you're ready," he said, opening the laptop that sat on the desk in front of him.

She picked up her pen, wrote the date at the top of a clean page, then pasted a smile on her face. "Ready."

He nodded, switched the recording equipment on and gave the date, time and her name. "Do you understand what illegal phone hacking entails?" he asked bluntly.

Seemed they were jumping right in. She straightened her spine. That suited her just fine. "Yes, I do."

"So you're confident you'd recognize phone hacking if you came across evidence that it had happened," he asked without hesitation and looking directly at her as if daring her to lie. If she wasn't mistaken, he was working from a list of questions on his laptop today. Perhaps this interview was more important than the first?

She leaned forward in her chair, her hands laced together and resting on the desk. "I believe I would."

"We already have evidence that ANS has been involved in illegal phone hacking. The evidence against former reporters Brandon Ames and Troy Hall is indisputable—they were caught on camera hiring hackers to record the phone and computer activity of Ted Morrow's and Eleanor Albert's families and friends. The only questions that remain are who else was involved, and who knew about it." There was something vaguely intimidating about the intelligence in his eyes, the determined jut of his chin, the perfect Windsor knot of his pale blue tie. This man would be a formidable adversary.

She arched an eyebrow. "Assuming someone else *was* involved or knew about it."

Not acknowledging her comment, his eyes flicked back to the laptop. "Do you work much with Angelica Pierce?"

Lucy kept her face neutral despite the distaste that rolled through her. *There* was a woman who was capable of something immoral, like phone hacking, if her treatment of her underlings was any gauge of her moral character. Angelica was mean, vain and selfish. But she wasn't here to talk about whom she personally did and didn't like, so she simply said, "I do a fair bit of background and preparation work for her."

"What about Mitch Davis?" Hayden flicked his pen over and under his fingers as he watched her. The man had an intensity in his gaze that was mesmerizing.

"Mitch has his own show, and he's a star at ANS. I rarely have a chance to speak to him directly." Mitch had been the one to announce the news of the president's illegitimate daughter at an inauguration gala, but Brandon and Troy had uncovered the information and given it to Mitch to reveal in a very public toast that put the new president on the spot. Those guys had given ambition a bad name with their slimy tactics, and they deserved the full force of the law—which they were now receiving. But as far as she was aware, they'd acted alone—other than blaming a casual researcher who'd already left ANS—and this witch hunt to try to implicate others in the pair's crimes was dangerous for everybody.

"Did you work with Brandon Ames or Troy Hall on their story about the president's daughter?"

She unscrewed the cap on her water bottle and took a sip, putting the cap back on before replying. He may have been asking the questions, but she was retaining a smidgeon of control over the process. "As I said when you asked the question two days ago, no, I didn't."

Barely acknowledging her reply, he pushed forward. "What about Marnie Salloway?"

"Marnie is an ANS producer and has the authority to assign me tasks," she said, making a list in her notebook of the names he was asking about. She wanted the record for when she reported back to Graham, but also to gain a little power in this meeting.

"Has she ever asked you to do anything illegal?"

"No."

"Anything involving phone hacking?"

"That would be illegal—" she smiled sweetly "—so my reply stands. No."

"Did you know that your stepfather and the president attended the same college at the same time?"

"Yes," she said. It was hardly a secret.

"Are you aware of any bad blood between them?"

Not apart from Graham thinking Ted Morrow had strutted around campus as if he owned it. "They didn't move in the same circles."

For another twenty minutes he grilled her, trying to trip her up, asking questions in different ways, expertly circling back over the line of questioning again and again. She had to admire his technique, but since she had nothing to hide, it was easy not to stumble.

When he paused to take a sip of water, she asked, "Hayden, do you honestly think someone else at ANS was involved in the hacking with Brandon and Troy, or are you fishing?"

"Someone else was involved," he said, his voice dropping a notch. His dark brown eyes burned with the intensity of his conviction.

Her fingers tightened around her pen. "Why are you so sure?"

"To start with, neither of them understood the process

well enough to have masterminded it. They were pawns, used by someone bigger."

She frowned as she followed his investigative reasoning. "I'm not someone bigger."

"No," he said slowly. His gaze locked on hers, taking on a speculative gleam and, as she understood his meaning, her stomach fell away.

"You're using me to get to Graham." She swallowed past an uncomfortable constriction in her throat. "I'm not here for routine questioning like the others. You think Graham ordered those goofballs to do it and that I know something that will implicate him."

One broad shoulder lifted, then dropped, as if this was a casual conversation, yet the intensity in his eyes didn't waver. "It's one theory."

A shiver ran down her spine. She'd known there was suspicion, of course. They all had. But if it was certain that someone else was involved, then ANS was in more trouble than she'd thought. They still had a bad seed in the company, and if Congress couldn't find who it was, they'd keep their focus on Graham. The exposé alone wouldn't save her stepfather. She had to do more.

She tapped a beat with the end of her pen on the desk as fragments of ideas flitted through her mind until one coherent plan formed.

She rested her forearms on the desk and leaned forward. "Hayden, I have a proposal for you."

He stilled. "I'm listening."

"If there truly is someone else in ANS who was involved in the hacking, and they were pulling Brandon and Troy's strings, then I want to know who they are, too. I can tell you now, it's not Graham. I know that man, and I know what he's capable of—he's not your guy. But the only way to prove that is to find the real culprit."

Hayden leaned back and folded his arms over his wide chest. "What exactly are you suggesting?"

"I'm going to help you with your investigation," she said, mind made up. "I can be your person on the inside. But I won't be involved in a witch hunt—this has to be evidence-based." She wouldn't be manipulated into finding circumstantial or misleading evidence against Graham.

"So you'll gather information for me?" He spoke slowly, as if testing the idea as he said it.

"Within reason. We have agree to some parameters first."

He cocked his head, brown eyes curious. "Your stepfather will be okay with you doing this?"

"I won't tell him just yet. It's possible he trusts someone he shouldn't, so for the time being, no one at ANS will know I'm assisting you." She felt a little queasy at the thought of keeping something of this magnitude from Graham, but in this case, the ends justified the means. The most important thing was that she was working in Graham's best interests.

Hayden rubbed a hand across a jaw darkened by five-o'clock shadow. "You believe in Boyle that much?"

"More."

He tapped one finger heavily on the desk three times, then blew out a breath. "Okay, I'm willing to give it a go and see how it pans out. But I have to warn you that I still think Boyle was involved, and I won't be dropping that line of inquiry just because you're helping."

"Noted." As soon as she found the person behind Troy and Brandon's crimes, Hayden's theory about Graham would be moot.

There was a sharp knock at the door. Hayden glanced

down at his watch. "Excuse me," he said, closing his laptop and striding across the room.

A neatly dressed woman in her thirties stood in the doorway behind a stroller containing a squirming Josh. Lucy felt her mouth curve into an unstoppable grin at the sight of the boy. He was gorgeous—Hayden's mini-me— and his expression was full of joy and delight.

"Daddy!" Josh squealed and reached out to his father.

"I'm sorry," the woman said. "I didn't realize you were still busy. Would you like me to keep him longer?"

Hayden reached down and lifted his son high, planting a kiss on top of his head. "No, we're almost done. I'll take him."

"Okay." The nanny leaned forward and said goodbye to her charge. The image of the three of them was so beautiful in that moment that Lucy felt an aching hollowness spread through her middle. They looked like a family.

After closing the door behind the nanny, Hayden wheeled the empty stroller across the room with Josh in one arm. When Josh saw Lucy, his face lit up, then he looked frantically around the room. "Goggie!" he demanded.

"Hello, Josh," she said on a laugh. "Rosebud is asleep in her basket at home."

Josh's little bottom lip pushed out for a split second— until he noticed how close his father's face was, and began to pat his cheeks. Despite flinching at one of the pats that hit his eye, Hayden pushed the stroller into a corner. "If you can give me five minutes, I'll set Josh up in his playpen with a few toys and we can continue," he called over his shoulder.

"Sure," she said. He opened the door to one of the suite's bedrooms and Lucy slipped out of her chair to follow—partly because it was a great chance to look for more clues for the assignment Graham had given her on Hayden, and partly out of curiosity.

At the park yesterday, she'd carried Josh most of the time and played with him, so she hadn't had much of a chance to observe father and son together. This evening, with Hayden setting his son up in the playpen, asking him which toys he'd like, she could see more clearly. And there was something a little…awkward about the interaction. Her gaze drifted around the room. Sitting on top of an end table was a haphazard pile of baby manuals, one thick tome perched on the top, open and spine up, its pages dog-eared. Perhaps Hayden was floundering now that he was a single father? She glanced back to man and son, her heart clenching tight for them both, for all they'd lost. For all they were dealing with now.

"He's a beautiful boy, Hayden." An acknowledgment of that truth wasn't much, but it was all she could offer him. "So precious."

Hayden looked down at Josh, who chose that moment to give a wide, toothless grin. "Yeah, he is," he said softly.

A bright, sparkling idea formed in her mind—a way to get more time with Hayden and his son. She squeezed her hands together and told herself she needed that time because Hayden had his guard down more when his son was there, so her subtle digging for information for the exposé was easier. But she was uneasily aware that she wanted to spend more time with the males in the Black family. She just hoped to high heaven that it wouldn't influence her professional judgment.

"I know a park that's the best place to feed the ducks," she said. "I was thinking, since you're not from D.C., you might be looking for places to take Josh. Rosebud and I could show you on the weekend if you want."

His fingers stilled against the top of the playpen, where they'd been tapping. "Lucy, I don't—"

"No problem if you'd rather not. I just thought Josh might get a kick out of seeing the ducks. There's a great playground there, too. And I'll be taking Rosie on the weekend anyway, so it's no bother," she said, aware she was babbling now.

He wrapped a hand around the back of his neck as he watched his son for endless moments. The expression on his face was so tender, so filled with love, it was heart-breaking. Eyelashes of darkest brown lay in a fan, almost resting on his cheeks as he gazed down.

He shook his head slowly. "Lucy, it's inappropriate to socialize with you."

"What if we use the time to plan what I'll be looking for at ANS?" she said as she tucked her hair behind her ear. "A briefing for your spy, so to speak, and Josh gets an outing as a bonus."

He scrubbed his hands through his hair, then let them rest low on his hips. "Okay, sure. But bring pen and paper, because we will be working."

A burst of nervous anticipation skittered up her spine. He'd agreed. Part of her hadn't believed he would—the same part that wondered now if she'd bitten off more than she could chew. Wondered if spending a day in a social setting with Hayden—and all his brooding testosterone—was akin to playing with fire.

She bit down on her lip. No, this would be fine. It was still a good plan. The best plan she had. Plan A.

She drew in a full breath and tried to calm her racing heart. "You can pick me up Sunday morning. Say, ten?"

"Ten's fine." A faint frown line formed between his brows, showing he wasn't convinced he should have accepted. He wasn't alone.

She glanced around for a piece of paper. "I'll write down my address for you. It's not far from—"

"I know where you live," he said, his voice a low, solemn rumble.

"Of course you do," she said wryly—he probably knew more about her than many of her friends did. Having spent her first eleven years living with her media magnet of a father in something of a fishbowl, she preferred now to be the one controlling the news story—the journalist instead of the target. So it was surprising that Hayden doing background research on her didn't worry her as much as she would have predicted. There was something strangely safe, something honorable and decent about Hayden Black, despite his investigation's potential for disaster for her family.

He guided her out of the bedroom with its playpen, toward the desk where he'd been grilling her just a few minutes ago. "We'll wrap it up here for today."

She gathered her things and tucked them in her bag, glad to have a task to hide how restless her hands suddenly were. "I'll see you Sunday," she said and looked back at Hayden. His forehead was lined and she felt cold apprehension filling her veins. She hesitated, and he opened his mouth to say something, but before he could cancel, she turned and slipped out the door.

Two days later, Lucy sat with Hayden on the shady banks of the Potomac River, a sleeping boy on a blanket between them. They'd fed the ducks, strolled around and now, as Josh was recouping his energy, Lucy and Hayden had fallen into an *almost* comfortable silence. From the moment he'd picked her up, it was as if they'd both been warily circling the social component of the day. Hayden had been unfailingly polite, if distant, and she'd followed suit. In the past, her social skills had been strong enough to cope with conversing with the rich, the royal, the famous and the powerful. But those same social skills faltered with Hayden Black. They'd mainly talked to, or about, Josh.

It wasn't just the investigation—though that was enough to make things less than comfortable between them—it was the unfailing awareness she had of him as a man. She could *feel* where he was, and when he'd been close she could smell the masculine musk of his skin. She'd lost the trail of something Josh had been saying more than once because she was paying more attention to his father at her side. And there were still those unguarded words she'd said the last time they'd been in a park together that were hanging between them—she was no closer to knowing what he thought about them.

Though there were a few things she did know more about now. The digging she'd done for the exposé in the past two days had focused on his company—it seemed working in the security business was lucrative. Or it was if you were as good as Hayden Black. The company he'd started only a few years ago now took in several million dollars in fees a year, and his personal wealth was estimated to be in the millions and growing. He'd come a long way from the boy who'd put himself through law school on a military scholarship and worked as an investigative lawyer in the military police until his time in the armed forces was up. Now he was a wealthy single father of a one-year-old.

She looked down at the sleeping boy, his face flushed a faint pink, remembering the trace of awkwardness she'd seen the night Hayden had set him up in the playpen. That image had worried at the edges of her mind. She moistened her lips and dared a personal question. "Has it been hard becoming his sole parent?"

Hayden's head snapped up, surprise in his eyes. Then he leaned back on his hands and nodded wearily. "The hardest thing I've ever done."

If they were going to get into a deeper conversation, she should be looking for clues to skeletons in his professional career for her exposé, or evidence of bias, yet she couldn't help prodding a little further into his relationship with Josh. "Did your wife do most of the care before she died?"

He coughed out a bitter laugh. "Brooke didn't do much with him at all. Besides buy him designer clothes and show him off when she thought it would grant her social cachet." He pulled a cotton cover over his son and placed a hand protectively on the sleeping boy's back.

"So you looked after him?" She folded her legs up beneath her, turning to face Hayden more. This was the most personal information he'd disclosed and she was hungry for every detail, every expression.

"No," he said, wincing. "Brooke had staff for everything, including Josh. She—" He hesitated, obviously weighing how much information to share. She waited, letting the decision be completely his, though wishing she could ease the tension that bound his body tight. "She was a socialite from a very wealthy family who expected to be pampered. When we were first together, I was happy to oblige, but it turned out that she needed more pampering than a husband alone could give." His expression was wry, but it obviously veiled deeper emotions. "She had staff to clean the house, a chef, a personal trainer and from the day he was born, two live-in nannies for Josh, so they could work round the clock. He rarely saw his mother."

"Oh, Hayden." One of her father's sisters, Evelyn, lived

like that, but she could imagine nothing worse than out-sourcing her life, her son, so completely.

"I should have done something, been more involved." His voice was thick with self-recrimination, his face twisted with regret. "But Brooke said that children were her domain and she'd handle them the way she wanted. The way she'd been raised. And I hate to admit it, but I was sick of the arguments, so I let her have her way for some peace. For all our sakes, including Josh's. Besides, I was out of my depth—I'd never been a father before—how did I know the way she'd been raised was wrong?"

"I'm assuming that was quite different from the way you were raised," she said gently.

"You can say that again." He gazed down at Josh for a long moment before reaching out to smooth the hair back from his son's face. "I spent time with him when I could. Played with him at night, did things when I had a day off, but I guess part of me must have been okay with the way Brooke wanted things done or I would have changed them. Insisted." He rubbed two fingers across the deep lines on his forehead. "I was stupid."

"You seem to be making up for it now," she said.

He shook his head dismissively. "There's a long way to go before I become the type of father I want to be."

"I don't think you should be so hard on yourself." She reached over and laid a hand on the warm cotton covering his forearm, wanting to bring any comfort she could. "Josh clearly loves you, and he's happy. You're doing some-thing right."

"Thanks," he said with a half smile and glanced away. His expression was usually so serious that even a half smile seemed bright, drew her in till all she could see was him. His gaze dropped to the hand that still lay on his arm. When he looked back up to her, his coffee-brown eyes darkened, and his chest rose and fell too fast. She knew how he felt—suddenly this open park didn't contain enough oxygen. The strong muscles under her fingers burned with heat and held her hand trapped as if by magnetic force.

From what felt like miles away, Josh sighed in his sleep and curled his teddy in closer. Hayden stiffened and looked down at his son before jerking his arm away from her. Lucy blinked and blinked again, trying to reorient herself to the world around them. To the park. To the reality that she'd almost fallen under the spell of a man she needed to keep at arm's length. Of a man who would likely feel betrayed if he knew her real agenda in meeting him today.

Hayden cleared his throat. "Tell me why you're so good with Josh. You don't have any brothers or sisters, no young cousins or nieces or nephews. Is it just a natural thing with babies for you?"

She looked down at Josh, still holding his teddy close as he slept. If Hayden didn't already know her involvement with babies, his research would soon unearth it, especially as he already knew about the lack of children in her family. There was no reason not to tell him—it wasn't a secret, it was just something she normally didn't discuss. Yet…something deep inside her wanted him to understand this part of her.

"Before my father died," she began, still watching Josh, "he used to take me to volunteer at a residential home for people with disabilities that he'd established. He believed strongly that the wealth we'd been born to was a privilege, and it was our responsibility to help others. He also wanted me to stay in touch with how other people live."

"Sounds like he was a wise man."

She looked up to see if there was any other meaning behind his words—people occasionally grabbed the opportunity to take a sarcastic swipe about her father and his family, a consequence of their wealth and high profile. But Hayden's eyes held only interest in the story she was telling, and she was more grateful for that simple acceptance than she would have expected. She stretched her legs out in front of her, relaxing a fraction.

"After he died, my mother wanted to continue his mission with me. But she said I could choose my own charity—the residential home had been my father's passion."

"And being a typical ten-year-old girl, you chose babies," he said, stretching his legs out beside hers.

She bit down on her smile. "It was almost kittens."

He chuckled. "What did you do?"

"We set up a free clinic in North Carolina for mothers who are having a hard time with their new babies. It's staffed mainly by professionals—nurses, social workers and consulting doctors—and the moms and babies can stay a few nights, up to a week, to get help with feeding or getting their babies to sleep or whatever the problem is."

He tilted his head to the side as he regarded her. "That sounds like a great service."

"It is," she said, feeling a soft glow of pride filling her chest—those midwives were doing fabulous work. "When we moved to D.C., we set up another one here. I go in and hang around most weekends, just being an extra pair of hands. Sometimes it's babysitting while the new mom gets some rest, sometimes it's manning the phones."

Though helping out in person wasn't an act of charity—she loved those times. Being part of a team and helping to make a real difference in people's lives. She'd always thought of journalism as making a difference, too, but since the phone-hacking scandal had broken, she'd started to wonder.

Hayden reached into the picnic basket and offered her a strawberry. "Do you fund it on your own?"

She took the shiny red berry—her fingers practically sparking when they grazed Hayden's—and twirled it on its small stem. "It started with just me, but I'm working on getting Royall Department Stores involved and building more clinics throughout the country. Aunt Judith is already eager to help—I went to see her in Montana last year to discuss it, and we'll take the plan to the whole board soon."

"That's amazing," he said with simple but genuine respect in his voice, in his eyes. "You've created something that's made the world a better place."

A warm flush spread across her skin, and she smiled at him, basking in his approval, letting it soak through her. Then, with a start, she realized she'd let his opinion matter more than it should. She forced herself to look away. A harmless flirtation with Hayden was one thing. Melting inside because he'd approved of her charity work was quite another. This man was still running an investigation into ANS, and believed Graham was guilty. The last thing she needed was to become emotionally involved with Hayden Black.

She pulled her legs up and tucked them underneath her, and reminded herself of the rules.

Flirting, okay.

Emotional attachment, not okay.

She would just have to try harder to keep the line where it needed to be. Still, if she didn't remember, then Hayden probably would. He seemed to have a very firm grasp on where the lines should be.

And why did that thought rankle so much?

Four

Lucy dropped the strawberry back into the container and dusted her hands on her skirt. "So, about this investigation. What do you want me to do?"

Hayden didn't answer right away; he regarded her with that intense, steady gaze, as if he could see inside her soul and knew exactly what she was doing by changing the subject away from herself. Then he nodded once. "I'll be speaking to Marnie Salloway next, since she was the producer on the story that aired."

Lucy let out a relieved breath. They were back on solid ground instead of the slippery slope of potential emotional entanglement. "What about Angelica Pierce? Seeing as she was the journalist who fronted all the follow-up stories, she could be the one." She said the word *one* carefully—she might have accepted the probability that someone had helped Troy Hall and Brandon Ames, but there was no way there was a chain of people leading up to her stepfather. The sooner this investigation proved that, the better. But Hayden either didn't notice, or was choosing to ignore her inflection and its meaning.

"I'm not as worried about Angelica at this stage," he said, absently laying a hand on Josh as he slept on the blanket. "Or Mitch Davis for that matter, since both were handed the scripts—Mitch for the announcement at the inaugural ball and Angelica for the stories that followed. But Marnie is different. She could easily be the person who ordered the phone hacking, or filtered the order down from higher."

The gentle breeze from the river blew a strand of Lucy's hair across her face and she tucked it behind her ear as she watched him. "You're not worried I'll tip Marnie off?"

"Will you?" he asked, with only curiosity in his eyes—no trace of concern.

"No." She was on board with this project, believed in its goal to find the rat in ANS so she could protect Graham. Undermining it wasn't on the agenda.

"Even if you do, she'll find out in the morning when I call to make a time with her. And she has to be expecting that she's under suspicion, so I'm not telling you anything that's a state secret." His broad shoulders lifted then dropped in a casual shrug. "What's your take on Marnie?"

"This is off the record, right? Just background." Marnie would love an excuse to complain about her to Graham, to dig the knife in as deep as it would go, and Lucy would rather not give her the ammunition if she could avoid it.

"Off the record," he agreed.

She could say this directly or sugarcoat it, and she had a feeling Hayden would prefer plain speaking. "Marnie is rude and self-important."

His expression didn't alter, as if he'd been expecting as much. "She treats you badly?"

"She doesn't treat anyone below her well," she said, trying to be as balanced in her assessment as she could. "But she makes a special effort to make my life unbearable."

Something in his eyes changed, sharpened. "Is she the only one?"

"There's a club. They have T-shirts," she said with a half smile to cover the faint sting of rejection. It wasn't the first time in her life she'd found herself the target of others' thinly veiled jealousy or venom, and she knew it wouldn't be the last. She'd learned to not let it get to her a long time ago. Mostly she was successful at that.

"Have you told Graham?" he asked quietly.

Tell Graham? She almost laughed. Oh, yeah, that would go down well at the office. "Just because I'm related to the owner doesn't mean I can run to him when I have problems."

"Sounds to me like the opposite is happening. You're being treated worse because you're related to the owner." Deep frown lines appeared on his forehead. "Any other employee would have the right to complain about being harassed, so if you don't feel you can make that complaint, you're suffering discrimination."

"I'll be fine," she said and found a carefree smile. She didn't need his sympathy, or to have someone stand up for her. She was a big girl, in charge of her own life. Being a target of people like Marnie and Angelica was part and parcel of the privilege she'd been born to, nothing more, and she could handle it.

Hayden's head tilted to the side as he regarded her. "Did Graham offer you the junior reporter role?"

"He offered me a full-fledged reporter role. Then, when I turned it down, the weekend anchor job." Graham had just been trying to help, to give her a leg up in the industry.

The dear man had been baffled when she'd turned down the offers, but he'd grudgingly respected her decision.

"You'd make a good weekend anchor."

"No, I'd be okay as one." Being okay wasn't part of her career plan. "I want the role, sure. But when I get there, I want to be truly good."

"You're not what I expected," he said with the ghost of a smile on his lips.

"Neither are you," she admitted, though she wasn't sure what she had expected. Perhaps her experience with Angelica, Troy and Brandon had skewed her perception of investigators, but she hadn't been expecting Hayden to be as considered in his approach, as quietly perceptive. And she certainly hadn't expected the simmering chemistry between them. Even now, in the midst of a discussion about a congressional investigation, she could feel the almost visible haze of heat that filled the air whenever she was near him.

He cleared his throat. "So. Marnie. Could she have been involved?"

"Well, yes, she *could* have been involved." She'd tossed the same thought around a few times herself. "But just because she's horrible, and had the opportunity, that doesn't mean she *did* break the law."

He rubbed a hand across his chin. "From your insider's perspective, could Ames and Hall have obtained their information from phone hacking without Marnie knowing?"

"Sure, it's possible."

"Possible but unlikely?" he prompted.

She shrugged. "Unless you were suspicious that someone had illegal sources, it wouldn't be hard to be blindsided. Things happen in broadcast news so quickly that not everyone can be on top of everything."

He nodded slowly and she could almost see the cogs

turning in his mind. "It would be good if you could get me something on Marnie before I meet with her. Something that rattles her enough to admit to knowing."

She arched an eyebrow. "Assuming she was involved."

"Naturally," he said, one corner of his mouth quirking up.

She looked across at him, the investigator for Congress, the man who was haunting her dreams. And she started to wonder if she could say no to him about much at all. She held up her hands. "I'll see what I can do."

Dark had closed in when they pulled up in front of Lucy's row house, the only light coming from a nearby streetlamp that bathed them in a gentle glow. Her home had been something of a surprise—he would have guessed she'd live in a penthouse apartment within walking distance of cafés, not a place large enough for a family, painted in a rich cream. Every time he thought he had Lucy Royall pegged, she did something else to surprise him.

He shouldn't like that so much.

He shouldn't like *her* so much. No denying that he did, though. Couldn't wait to hear what she'd say next, what she'd do. When she was near, he found it hard to look at anything else—it was as if she had a golden glow about her, an aura of stardust. And that mouth—a generous cupid's bow that had driven him to distraction all day—every time she moistened those lips or pursed them in thought, heat had stroked down his spine. Keeping a professional distance was becoming more challenging by the hour.

He switched the car off and pulled on the hand brake. "Just let me get Josh out of the car seat and I'll walk you to your door."

"Don't disturb him. He's sleeping so peacefully," she said softly, turning to look at his son in the baby seat. "And don't lock him in either—just stay with him. It's about eight feet to my front door. Honestly, I'll be fine. I do it all the time."

Chivalry fought with fathering instincts—could he let a woman walk to her door alone, even if it was only a few steps away? But he looked at Josh in the rearview mirror, and fatherhood won. And perhaps avoiding a doorstep scene was wise—this might not be a date, but would he be able to resist kissing her?

He turned back to Lucy. "Once you're inside with the door locked, call my cell. I'll wait right here till I hear from you."

"That's very sweet," she said.

Sweet? He almost laughed. She wouldn't be saying that if she knew the thoughts that were currently bombarding him. Thoughts about the things he'd like to do with her, starting with peeling those clothes off her body, piece by piece. Underneath he knew she'd be luscious and petal-soft....

He cleared his throat and tried to clear his mind of its impure thoughts at the same time. It didn't work. Distraction, that was the key. He needed to say something, preferably about a neutral topic. "Thank you for today—Josh had a great time."

"I had a good time, too," she said, her voice barely more than a breath. Her mouth suddenly seemed so close, and he began to lean in before summoning his control and pausing. As she realized his intent, her pupils dilated. The pulse at the base of her throat fluttered like crazy. Still, he held—not leaning in farther, but not able to move away. Her moist, full lips were slightly parted, inviting him. A groan worked its way up from deep in his chest. Desire like this, that consumed, engulfed, had been absent from his life for a long time. He wanted nothing more than to give in to it, grasp it with both hands, to grasp *Lucy* with both hands and sink into the sensations she evoked in him.

But he couldn't let his guard down and think of her as a woman. He had an investigation to run and involvement with Lucy Royall would compromise his objectivity. Compromise him. He was ethically bound to keep emotional distance between them.

He clenched his jaw tight and leaned slow, excruciating inches back.

"Hayden?" she asked breathlessly.

He gripped the steering wheel until his fingers hurt, trying to anchor himself to something. "Yes?"

"Were you about to kiss me?"

His heart stuttered to a stop. He should have known Lucy wasn't the type of woman to let things lie, to choose the sensible path. "There was a moment, before I thought better of it," he admitted.

"I wish you had." She said the words softly, but there was no flirtation in them—they were honestly delivered and all the more powerful for it. Desire still tugged hard in the pit of his belly, demanding that he follow through and kiss her, but he couldn't give in. Wouldn't.

He muttered a curse and closed his eyes to limit the number of senses being assaulted at once. "Don't say that."

"But it's the truth," she said, her Southern accent thick. He opened his eyes in time to see her pink tongue peek out and moisten those lips that drove him crazy. "I've been wondering what kissing you would be like."

"Lucy, don't." There was a harshness in his voice that he hated, but was powerless to help. He was on the edge; every muscle vibrated with the effort of holding them still. If she pushed much further, he'd consign his ethics to hell and reach for her.

"What sort of kisser are you, Hayden?" She turned in the seat, facing him, pupils large in the dim light. "Soft and gentle? Strong and demanding?"

He groaned and banged his head back on the head-rest. Was she trying to kill him? "This can't happen," he growled. "I can't compromise my objectivity."

"What if I never tell?" Her voice was pure temptation, full of invitation and delicious promise, making his thundering heart thump even harder in his chest. For a moment, he wondered…could he? A shudder ripped through him. *Could he?* He glanced out the window, seeking a sign, maybe permission.

Instead he saw a fashionable D.C. street, and it struck him with the force of a blow.

D.C.

He was in this town to do a job. He'd been employed by *Congress,* damn it.

He scrubbed his hands down his face and refocused on what was important, then turned to Lucy to make sure she understood, as well. "*I'd* still know. And things would be different between us."

One corner of her mouth curved up into a half smile. "You don't think they'll be different after this conversation?"

"You'll notice I tried to stop this conversation before it started."

"Oops," she said and bit down on her lip, looking anything but sorry. "What should we do now?"

"Pretend it never happened." It was the only option left.

There was silence for long seconds as she watched him with a small line between her eyebrows. "And if I can't?"

"We don't talk about it." He slashed a hand down to

rest on his thigh, hoping he appeared more decisive than he felt. "Never let the topic come up again."

"Can you do that?"

"Yes." Sure, he could avoid *mentioning* it, but the look on her face now in the dim light of the car interior would be burned into his memory, and there was nothing he could do to avoid *thinking* about kissing her. Dreaming about it.

She picked up her hold-all handbag from the floor and held it close to her chest. "I should probably go inside."

"Yes," he croaked. Then he cleared his throat and tried again. "Yes, that would be best all around."

"Okay, then." She opened the car door with only a brief glance over her shoulder.

By sheer force of will, he let her walk up the three concrete stairs to her front door instead of drawing her back, keeping her beside him for even a few moments longer. Once she'd let herself in, he dropped his head to the steering wheel and cursed. He'd been stupid, *stupid* to let his guard down and consider kissing a key witness. What kind of investigator was he?

His cell phone rang and Lucy's number flashed on the screen. He drew in a fortifying breath and thumbed the talk button. "You're in?"

"Safe inside, with the door locked." Her voice was smooth velvet, enfolding him in the dim lamplight. His eyes drifted closed, shrinking his world down to just the cell at his ear and Lucy's voice.

"Good," he said, which was about all he could manage.

"Hayden, about that conversation we shouldn't have had…"

He knew he should hang up the phone now, knew he would regret this, but he couldn't stop himself from replying. "Yes?"

"I'm glad we did." He could just imagine her biting down on her luscious bottom lip as she paused, and his pulse spiked. "Though I would have been even happier if you had kissed me."

His head swam. *Hang up the cell, Black.*

He pinched the bridge of his nose and summoned his willpower. "Good night, Lucy."

"Night, Hayden."

He disconnected, threw the phone on the passenger seat and started the car. If he wasn't careful, this investigation might just kill him.

Three nights later, Lucy was in Hayden's suite, sitting cross-legged on one of the sofas, reams of paper, scribbled notes and printed photos spread around her. Hayden sat on the other sofa a few feet away, his long legs stretched in front of him, ankles crossed on the coffee table, going through a different pile of evidence.

Hayden glanced up at her, his hair haphazard from dragging his fingers through it. "Did you talk to the receptionists?"

Over the past three days, Lucy had spent time with everyone she could corner who worked in support roles at ANS—people who might have had the opportunity to notice things that didn't add up, and would have been treated badly by Marnie and her friends. Today she'd asked Graham's secretary, Jessica, to have lunch with her and the other executive assistants, after telling her that being Graham's daughter was making it hard to make friends.

"I heard a lot of gossip about who's sleeping with whom—I had no idea it was that much like a college dorm."

His eyebrow quirked. "Any interesting connections?"

"Why? Fancy someone at ANS?" she asked with as much innocence as she could muster.

The heat that had been lurking in his eyes for three days blazed to life, but his voice was even. "I was thinking in terms of the investigation. Which you knew."

She did know, but flirting with Hayden Black was dangerously alluring. Like touching a naked flame.

"If we're talking about the investigation, then apparently Marnie had a fling with Mitch Davis. Since we don't think Mitch had anything to do with the story besides being handed the toast to give at the inauguration ball, it's probably not relevant."

"Ames or Hall sleeping with anyone?"

"Brandon Ames was seeing one of the accountants, but she dumped him when she found out what he'd done. And I'm not sure if an accountant would have been much use with phone hacking, so I doubt she was involved."

"Hall?" he asked, leaning forward.

"No one had heard anything. If he was seeing someone, it was probably outside ANS."

Hayden swore under his breath. "Maybe it was too much to hope for a sexual link to lead us to the other perpetrators. But thanks for trying."

"I've made friends with one of the custodians—or rather, Rosebud has—and I'm hoping to run into her tomorrow night again. She might know something about any late-night meetings that other people wouldn't notice."

"Rosebud comes in handy," he said dryly, and she wondered if he realized she'd used Rosie to start a conversation that first day in the park.

She smiled noncommittally. "She sure does."

Connections with other journalists came in handy, too—she'd heard back this morning from a friend she'd graduated with who'd gone on to work for a New York newspaper. Lucy had asked him to poke around and see if he could find any secrets in Hayden's past for Graham's exposé. Her friend had dug up someone who knew Hayden's in-laws. Seemed they weren't his biggest fans. They'd wanted their daughter to marry someone of her own class, not a boy—then in the military—who'd come from nowhere. The only thing they were happy about was that he'd put the money he'd inherited from his deceased wife into a trust fund for Josh. Nothing particularly explosive for the story, but her background research folder was growing.

Lucy sifted through more of the papers around her, documents she'd already read, searching for an evasive clue, until Hayden looked up sharply.

"Did you know Angelica wears contacts?"

"Doesn't surprise me, but no." And now that she thought about it, Angelica's eyes were an unusual shade of blue—almost aqua.

He laid down the papers in his hand and picked up his coffee mug. "Why doesn't it surprise you?"

"She's vain, and very careful about letting anyone see her unless she's wearing a full face of makeup. The other on-air journalists are always immaculately presented when they go on camera, but off air they're more casual."

He returned the mug to the coffee table. "It probably doesn't mean anything. I just don't trust her."

"Well, I sure don't trust her," Lucy said. She'd seen her being nasty and vindictive—experienced it herself—far too many times for that. "Do you think she could be involved?"

"Could be, but it's unlikely." There was a definite note of frustration in his voice. "If she'd found the leads, would she let Ames and Hall take the credit? She's ambitious and it was the biggest story of the year—surely she'd want her name attached."

He was right, which left them back at square one. Well, not exactly square one, because they'd eliminated some leads. Putting her hands in the small of her back, she stretched, trying to get rid of some of the kinks that sitting on the sofa had created. From the corner of her eye she noticed Hayden subtly watching and her pulse picked up speed. She turned her head a fraction, just enough to let him know she'd noticed. He didn't look away. If anything, his gaze intensified. Her mouth dried and she moistened her lips—he watched that, too. Then, oh, so slowly, he drew in a breath and looked away, dissolving the tension that had risen. She steadied herself and followed his lead. Falling under Hayden Black's thrall was a bad, bad idea for her sanity.

What was she supposed to be doing? The investigation. Who else could have been helping Troy and Brandon if it wasn't Angelica. Right.

She rubbed her hands over her face, hoping it would help her focus. "If someone else is involved, it makes more sense that they're more senior, not just another reporter."

He riffled through a pile of reports until he found a chart she'd drawn two nights ago. "Tell me again about who was supposed to be managing Ames and Hall."

She scooted over to his sofa and looked at the chart illuminated in soft lamplight. Heat emanated from his body. "This is the line of responsibility." She reached across and touched a fingertip to the paper he held, and as she did, the sensitive underside of her wrist grazed lightly over crisp hairs on his forearm. A shiver ran up her spine.

She heard a sharply indrawn breath and looked to see his gaze locked on her, his eyes darkened with the same need she felt. For a charged moment, neither of them moved, and the only sound she heard was the pounding of her heart. He was so close—a whisper away.

"Lucy, we can't." His voice was torn from his throat.

Hearing he was as close to the edge as she was had the opposite effect from what he'd intended. She'd never been good at following rules, or doing what she was told. The day's stubble on his cheeks beckoned, and she ran her fingertips across it to see what it felt like, what *he* felt like. His jaw was clenched so hard that a muscle in the corner jumped.

"I've been wondering what it would feel like to touch you," she said, watching the path her fingers traveled over his jaw. "In fact, I wished for it."

He winced as if in pain. "You should be more careful about what you wish for."

"I was careful," she murmured. Her fingertips feathered along the strong column of his throat. "I'm wishing for it again right now."

He stilled, his only movement the rapid rise and fall of his chest. "I swear, Lucy, you'd try the patience of a saint." His gaze fell to her lips. "And I hate to admit it, but I'm no saint." Finally, his hands crept under her hair to cradle the nape of her neck, lightly massaging, sending a spray of fireworks across her skin.

"No regrets yet," she said, though she wasn't sure her voice was strong enough for him to hear. He leaned in, his body tense, and his lips brushed across hers, the softest of caresses, yet enough to leave her trembling.

"Hayden," she whispered with all the need inside her. A shudder ripped through his body. He pulled her flush against him and kissed her, the warm pressure of his mouth like nothing she'd ever felt. When his tongue moved against hers, the shimmering heat exploded inside her, and she crawled onto his lap. It still wasn't close enough. At last, after all these days of hoping and nights of dreaming, Hayden was kissing her. Hungrily. Gloriously. And she was melting.

On a groan, he wrenched his mouth away and they both gasped to find their breath again, but she didn't stop touching. Couldn't. The skin on his neck, below where the stubble ended, was surprisingly smooth and oh, so warm. She pushed her fingers down past the collar of his shirt, wanting nothing more than to feel the strength of his shoulders, to know how they'd taste. But before she could make much headway, he brought her mouth back to his.

"This is a bad idea," he murmured, lightly kissing the edges of her lips, lingering at the corner of her mouth.

He ironed a hand down her back and her pulse jerked erratically. "A very bad idea," she agreed with a catch in her voice.

"But damned if I don't want to do it anyway." He cupped her face and the fine tremor that ran through his hands created an answering shiver that spread through her whole body.

"Oh, yes. Me, too," she moaned.

He cursed under his breath, then gave a rueful half laugh. "I was hoping you'd be the sensible one."

She caught his earlobe between her teeth and gently nipped. "There's no fun in being sensible all the time."

"I'm beginning to see that," he said as he laid her down on the sofa, pressing her into the cushions with his body. He kissed along her throat. "But if we do this—"

"If?" she said incredulously, desire scorching along her skin at every point Hayden's body touched hers.

He lifted his weight on hands that rested at either side of her head. "If we do this, we have to agree on a couple of ground rules first."

"Anything." She reached for him, trying to get him to bring his delicious heat back.

He didn't move. "I'm serious, Lucy."

"I can see that," she conceded on a sigh and wriggled to sit up. Seemed they were having a conversation whether she wanted to or not.

Five

"So, ground rules," Lucy said, her hands pressing against Hayden's chest as they sat entwined on the sofa. For the moment, ignoring her body's insistent straining toward him was her best option so they could get the talking part of the night over as quickly as possible. Then they could get back to the part where he was kissing her. She went a little dizzy just thinking about it.

He swallowed hard and she watched the progress of his Adam's apple, up then down. "This can only be a one-time deal."

She slid the first button of his shirt through the buttonhole. "Sure." She wasn't thinking ahead; she was too busy being smack-dab in the middle of the moment, so if he thought she'd put up an argument about some future possibility, he was wrong.

His hands were motionless on her hips, but his fingers dug in, his heart thumping so hard she could feel it through his shirt. "No one can know."

"I won't breathe a word." She released a second and third button. A fourth. A whorl of dark hair peeked through the opening she'd made, teasing her. Daring her.

"And," he rasped, "we both promise not to use it against the other if things get sticky with the investigation."

She paused a beat and met his gaze. "We wouldn't do that."

His dark brows drew together until they almost met. "You don't know I wouldn't use it to my advantage."

"I know." Hayden Black was a man made of honor. And *heat*. The burning imprints of his hands held her hips in place beside him on the sofa, much too far away. Why didn't he pull her closer?

"Agreed?" His voice was tight, his gaze locked intently on her.

"Agreed," she said, barely caring what she agreed to, as long as it led to more of his bone-melting kisses.

He pulled her against him and his mouth met hers, giving all that heat to her at last. Her throat hummed with a sound of sheer pleasure and she twined her arms around his neck, unwilling to give him the chance to break away again. She'd wanted him in this exact position for days, and the reality was living up to every single fantasy. The hunger. The solid muscle under her hands, the taste of his lips. Sizzling energy rushed through her veins, melting her from within.

When they broke apart for air, there was a flare of satisfaction in his eyes, and it sent a shiver skating across her skin.

"Lucy," he said, his voice almost reverential, yet thick with need. "I've wanted you so badly, I thought I'd go crazy with it."

She smiled, glad she wasn't the only one who'd been

stuck in that place of torment. "I haven't been able to think straight since I met you."

Groaning, he pulled her onto his lap and she wrapped around him, knees on either side of his thighs, pressing as close as she could with layers of fabric between them. She found the thick ridge of his need and pressed into him even more.

Swiftly, he undid her buttons and peeled her top back, kissing the tops of her shoulders as he exposed them and sliding the fabric down her arms before wadding it into a ball and throwing it across the room.

"Your skin is like cream," he said against the curve of her neck. "Smooth and delectable."

In one fluid move, he unhooked her bra and threw it in the direction of her top. The cool air nipped at her naked breasts, but the simmering intensity in his eyes more than compensated. Hot fingers trailing her collarbone slipped lower, and his mouth followed them down. She arched back, her mind full of him; nothing could penetrate her thoughts but Hayden and his exquisite torture of her senses. When his lips closed over the peak of her breast, she speared her fingers across his scalp, loving the slide of his hair over the sensitive skin between her fingers. Loving what his mouth was doing even more.

One of his large palms encircled her breast, squeezing ever so gently, and her eyes drifted closed to absorb the full effect of the magic he was wreaking.

"They're some impressive skills you have there," she said on a ragged breath.

"All driven by desperate need for you," he growled.

His shirt was hanging open, yet concealing far too much of him. She pushed the open sides over his shoulders and down his arms until he flicked the shirt off completely. With a ragged moan, she spread her hand over the planes of his chest, reveling in the feel of crisp dark hair under her fingertips, greedy for as much of him as she could touch. She scraped her teeth across his biceps, feeling his shudder as it ripped through his body. It was too much, but not enough.

His hand snaked down between their bodies and released her trouser button and zipper, and when his fingers slid over the exposed satin, she bucked her hips to meet them. She'd never been this crazed with desire before. Being with Hayden was beyond her wildest dreams.

He twisted and laid her back onto the sofa, the fabric smooth and luxurious against her bare skin, and he loomed over her, breathing heavily. Time slowed as she took in the sight of him, of the masculine beauty that was all hers tonight. She'd never forget the way he looked in this moment, the way he'd made her feel. A ripple seemed to run through the air and she knew this was a memory that would last her entire life—a defining moment, a turning point. Nothing would ever be the same again. Nothing.

"Hayden," she whispered, and suddenly the world started again as he leaned down to capture her lips, kissing her deeply, hungrily, sliding his tongue against hers. She wrapped her legs around his waist and arched up into him, savoring the feel of his body pressed against her. He ground into her and every cell in her body came alive with an electric current, vibrating and sparking.

Then Hayden stilled and heaved in a breath. "That bottomless bag of yours has got to have condoms."

Delicious sensation came to a screeching halt and she blinked up at him. Protection? "No," she said slowly, mentally running through the contents of her bag. "You don't have any?"

He swore under his breath and wrenched himself away. "No idea, but I'm hoping like crazy." He ditched his jeans and strode to the bathroom, disappearing through the door, leaving Lucy to run through the options. One of them could sprint to the drugstore. A possibility, but it was a long time to be separated in their current state. She glanced at the lights of the city twinkling through the window across the room—she didn't want to leave this suite alone for anything less than a fire. They could both make a mad dash to her place—she had some condoms in a drawer. No, Josh was asleep, they couldn't leave. They could ring the concierge and see if he kept a supply—

Hayden reappeared—fully sheathed—with a predator's grin and prowled across the room. She managed to ditch her trousers and panties by the time he reached her, anticipation singing through her entire body.

"Thank goodness," she said as he climbed back on the sofa and covered her with all that heat. "I was making contingency plans and they were getting more ridiculous by the second."

"I look forward to hearing about those plans," he said, nipping at her earlobe. "Later."

"Much later," she said. "I have other plans for our mouths right now."

Never slow on the uptake, Hayden kissed her, nipping, sucking, stroking until her head swam and she was writhing underneath him.

"Now," she begged. "Please, now."

After drawing out the moment for several more agonizing seconds, he captured her gaze and slid into her in one smooth, deep stroke. The world swirled around her and came alive. *She* came alive. She tightened her grip on his waist with her legs, holding him there, savoring the sensation. Then, despite her hold, he began to move, and she was lost to the dance of their bodies, helpless to do anything but match his rhythm and give in to the sensations.

She soared higher than the stars, and Hayden's voice at her ear telling her she was beautiful, that she felt incredible, sent her higher still. The rhythm they created together was pure magic; her body was sparkling with bright, pulsing energy. His deep murmurs at her ear became more intense, edgier, pushing her to the brink, and she dug her fingers into his back, holding on, wanting the moment to last. His thrusts became faster, more urgent, and a wave of pleasure rose within her, too big to be contained, and she cried out his name as it burst in an explosion of color and light and intensity, dimly aware that Hayden followed her soon after.

Hayden stared at the ceiling from his position on the sofa, Lucy wedged beside him, his stomach slowly hollowing out. That had to be the stupidest thing he'd ever done, which was saying something, because he'd done a lot of stupid things in his life.

Making love to Lucy had been earth-shattering, yes. Bone-melting, definitely—he might not be able to stand again for a week. But still stupid.

What exactly were those rules beforehand meant to achieve, other than to give him a false sense of security and permission to sleep with her? He liked Lucy—maybe too much—but she was still lying to cover for her stepfather, and had pretty much admitted she'd do anything to save Graham Boyle.

Hayden had no doubt Lucy had genuinely wanted him tonight—the need in her eyes had been a thing of beauty. But would she use what had happened between them against him to protect Boyle, if she felt she had no other choice? His gut clenched tighter. He'd like to think not, but obviously his judgment was seriously impaired when it came to her.

Even if she wasn't lying to protect her stepfather, she was ten years younger, for Pete's sake. He'd been twenty-two once, with all the fun and experimentation that entailed. But he was thirty-two now, with a son. Lucy and he were in completely different places in their lives. He winced and called himself a few more versions of idiot.

The wisest move was probably to step down from the investigation and hand it over to someone else in his company. He now had a conflict of interest. But he was so close to finding the key to this case, and a new investigator would take time to get up to speed. That time could be the difference in catching Boyle and letting him slip through a hole in the net. No, as long as he kept his distance from Lucy now and didn't let it affect his integrity as an investigator, then staying on was the best thing for the case.

Lucy stirred beside him and leaned up on one elbow, a drowsily satisfied smile on her face. "Under different circumstances—" she said, and he cut her off.

"Under different circumstances it still would have been a one-time deal." He said it as gently as he could—despite it being the truth, it wasn't the best etiquette to reject a woman right after making love to her.

Undeterred, Lucy tilted her head to the side. "I thought it went well. Granted, it might have been better had we made it to the bed, and things did get a little carried away toward the end there, but you have to admit that parts of it were glorious."

His skin shivered with the memory of how good it had been. "Lucy, all of it was glorious." He cupped the side of her face in his palm. "There wasn't a millisecond that wasn't glorious."

She laid a hand over his as he stroked her cheek, confusion in her hazel eyes. "But you wouldn't want me again if things were different."

Wouldn't want her? "Oh, sweetheart, I'd have to be dead not to want you again." He withdrew his hand, feeling the loss of her warm skin. "But my life is a mess. I'm all Josh has now—he deserves a parent who's focused on him. And any attention I have free needs to be on my business. I've let things slide a little since becoming a single father, so this investigation is important to my career. I just don't have time to experiment with relationships."

One dark blond eyebrow jumped up. "I haven't asked you for forever."

"I know." He scrubbed a hand through his hair and tried to regroup—he was making a mess of this, as well. "I'm sorry. This is my fault—I should never have let it happen."

"There were two of us on this sofa, Hayden," she said with a touch of impatience and sat up.

"But one of us thinks being sensible is overrated," he pointed out. "I thought so, too, at your age. Which is why I needed to be the one who was thinking about consequences tonight."

She stilled and her eyes turned to ice. "That won't be a problem again." She stood and began collecting her clothes.

He thumped his head back on the armrest—hard. He'd basically called her a child. Could he have created a bigger disaster of the night if he'd tried? "Lucy—"

"No, you're right," she said as she threw on her blouse, then stepped into her trousers. "We were irresponsible. It won't happen again."

She was at the door before he'd gathered enough wits—or pants—to respond. He strode across the room, still buttoning his jeans, and laid a palm on the door above her head, shutting it. She leaned her forehead against the door, her fingers still gripping the handle.

"Lucy, I've botched this." Understatement of the year, but his brain still wasn't working at full capacity after the best sex he could remember.

She didn't lift her head. "Yes."

"No, don't spare my feelings," he said wryly.

A soft, reluctant laugh floated up from where her face was hidden against the door, followed by a sigh. "What do you want me to say, Hayden? You wanted it to be a one-time deal. Well, I'm on my way out the door, with no intention of allowing a repeat. You got your wish. So why are you stopping me?"

"I want things to be right between us. I don't want you to leave now with things this screwed up." He was normally good at smoothing things over with people, at allaying their concerns. It was a skill that came in handy during investigations. Yet after crossing boundaries he'd set for himself and sleeping with Lucy Royall, he'd managed to insult her. Things had now veered outside his area of expertise. His temples throbbed. In truth, things had left his area of expertise some time ago.

He looked down at her blond head leaning against the white door and cursed himself. He liked Lucy and he'd never forgive himself if he let her walk out of here hurt.

"You said you'd help with the investigation," he said slowly. "That won't happen if you walk out that door now."

She tucked her hair behind her ears then turned to look up at him with a wobbly smile. "Things are fine between us."

Cupping her shoulders to steady them both, he peered into her eyes, seeking evidence that she was telling the truth. "You're sure?"

She shot him a rueful look. "One hundred percent."

"Prove it." He stepped back, letting her go if she

wanted, hoping like all hell she didn't. If she slipped through that door, she'd take all the warmth from the room with her.

She didn't leave, instead eyeing him warily. "How do you suppose I prove it?"

"Have a normal conversation with me. You have to give evidence to Congress tomorrow—you need to be in top form for that. We should discuss it."

"Thanks for the offer, but I'll be all right. I'll stick to the truth and we won't have any trouble," she said, repeating his words from their first meeting with a small smile.

He let out a relieved breath. "That's always a good policy."

"Will you be there?"

"At the back of the room, so you probably won't see me. I'll give you a call in the afternoon."

"Talk to you then," she said, and this time when she opened the door and slipped out, he let her go despite the pressure in his chest.

Lucy stepped into a cab and gave the driver the address of the ANS offices. She'd just finished giving evidence to the congressional hearing and was exhausted and needed a muffin, preferably chocolate chip, but Graham would be waiting to hear how it went. She sat back in the seat and leaned her head back, the questions they'd asked and her answers rolling around in her head.

One question in particular kept repeating.

"Have you heard the name Nancy Marlin?"

She'd said no, but the name kept coming back into her mind, as if there was a memory just out of reach. She closed her eyes, let out a long breath and tried to clear her mind of everything except the name.

It hovered, she could almost see it…then she plucked it from her memory. Her eyes popped open and she grabbed her cell, dialing Hayden's number on instinct.

"You did well," he said when he picked up.

She almost smiled at the warm approval in his voice but stopped herself in time—the time had come for emotional distance from Hayden Black. It should have been a priority last night—no, from day one—but it was even more important since they'd made love. Sleeping with him while she was working on Graham's exposé had been a monumental mistake. It was likely that Hayden would find the person behind the phone hacking before Graham set an air date on the exposé, but if Hayden found out in the meantime that she'd worked on it even after they made love, he'd have a right to feel betrayed. He'd find the culprit in time, she had no doubt. And in the meantime, emotional distance was the key. She set her shoulders.

"Where are you now?" she asked as she checked out the window for her own location.

"In the corridor outside Senator Tate's office."

"I've remembered something else."

His voice immediately changed, became 100-percent business. "I'll meet you at my hotel in fifteen."

She pictured his hotel room as it had been last night—strewn with their clothes, their naked bodies sprawled on the sofa. The blood in her veins began to heat. Then she remembered how she'd left and her blood went ice-cold. Maybe she shouldn't have called him now.

"Lucy?"

No, she'd done the right thing to call. Hayden was the investigator for Congress—the exact person she should tell. They just had to meet somewhere private that wasn't his hotel.

"My place has muffins, let's meet there," she said.

"My hotel. I'll pick up muffins on the way," he said and disconnected.

When Hayden arrived at his suite, Lucy was already there, looking as she had on the screen when he'd watched her give evidence—conservative mint-green dress, her hair scraped back and pinned at the nape of her neck. And now, as then when he'd seen her, his pulse galloped along like a wild horse with no intention of being tamed.

He tossed her a paper bag that was fragrant with the scent of freshly baked muffins, and unlocked the door. "As promised."

"You're a prince among men, Hayden Black."

He threw his keys and wallet on a side table and turned to find her already making headway with the first muffin. She seemed comfortable enough given the nature of their meeting, and it filled him with relief. After the way things had ended last night, he'd feared she might not return his calls, or agree to see him with anything short of a subpoena. But thankfully things appeared to be okay between them, if a little awkward. Now all he had to do was not cross any lines with her again. Never let his guard down.

He grabbed his notebook and sat at the desk. "First, tell me you didn't remember this when you were in front of Congress and keep it from them."

"No, in the cab afterward," she said, taking the other chair at the desk. "But it was their question that made me remember."

"Which question?"

"They asked if I'd heard of Nancy Marlin."

"And you said no." He'd been taking notes through all the hearings, but he didn't need to check the notes from Lucy's testimony—he remembered every word.

She nodded, she was practically vibrating with restless energy. "But the name bugged me and I remembered in the cab on the way back to work. I overheard a conversation months ago where the name came up."

"Who was talking?"

"Marnie Salloway and Angelica Pierce."

The wheels in his mind began to turn. This could be the piece of the puzzle that made all the others fit together.

"Who is Nancy Marlin?" she asked.

"A friend of Barbara Jessup." When the president was young, his family had employed Barbara Jessup as a maid—the list of questions for the hearing had included random names of people connected to the president, even by two or three degrees of separation. There was only one reason journalists could have to be talking about a maid's friend.

Lucy's eyes widened. "This is it."

Part of him agreed with her—this *could* be it—but he didn't want to count his chickens and jinx it. He drew in a measured breath. "Do they know you overheard them?"

"I doubt it. I was in the supply closet and they stopped just outside the door. Once I had what I wanted, I waited for them to finish—with Marnie and Angelica, keeping a low profile is essential to survival."

Having met Angelica, he understood. "I want you to repeat word for word what they said."

"At first they were complaining about one of the other producers, then Angelica asked, 'Is there any progress with Nancy Marlin?' Marnie said, 'Not yet, but we're still trying.' And Angelica said, 'Keep me up to date.' After that, they went their separate ways and I sneaked out and back to my desk."

A buzz of excitement was growing in his blood. He'd finally found it. "They're both involved," he said, staring down at the conversation he'd just copied onto paper. "They've hacked into Barbara Jessup's phones."

"Do you want to tell Congress to call me back?"

"We might have to, but I'll try with Ames and Hall first. One overheard conversation isn't much to go on, but if I can get them to give Marnie and Angelica up, they might be able to give me more evidence so the charges will stick."

She put the remains of her second muffin back in the bag and brushed the crumbs from her fingers. "Wouldn't they have given them up already if they were going to?"

"If they think we're onto Marnie and Angelica anyway and it's only a matter of time before we gather enough evidence, then they might try to negotiate with whatever they have on them. I can also interview Marnie and Angelica again, telling them that this conversation was overheard. It might be enough for one of them to panic or slip up."

With a restless move of her shoulders, she glanced out his window. "I wish I'd remembered earlier."

"Remembering at all is great." Gently, he turned her back to face him. "I'll try and keep your name out of it if I can."

Her eyes flashed fire. "Our ground rules said we wouldn't let our involvement interfere with the investigation. Don't try to protect me."

"I'd do what I could to protect any witness. If I can get stronger evidence, then we won't need yours and there's no point putting you in the line of fire. If we need you, don't worry," he said, cupping the side of her face, "I'll put you back before Congress without blinking."

As he'd hoped, his words had coaxed a reluctant smile from her.

"As long as you had more of these muffins, I'd be okay." Her smile faded and she picked up her red hold-all bag. "I have to get back to the office. Graham's waiting to hear how it went."

He handed her the leftover muffins. "Are you going to tell him about Marnie and Angelica?"

"I'll have to. They're his employees," she said, her gaze on the paper bag she'd accepted from him.

The cynical part of his brain was still sure she was covering for her stepfather. Graham Boyle was at the top of this chain of deceit, Hayden had no doubt. What he wasn't sure about was whether Lucy's willingness to help with the investigation was part of her plan to ensure she was on the scene once he found the evidence on Graham. Perhaps she even hoped to influence him into discarding that evidence.

He hated thinking that way, wished he could just be open with her, but he had to be realistic. Her information had been invaluable so far, but she was an employee of ANS and Graham Boyle's stepdaughter. Her loyalty would always be with him. Hayden understood that. Didn't mean he couldn't protect his investigation where he could.

"Don't tell him yet. Come back tonight after work and we'll make a plan for interviewing Marnie and Angelica again. I'll see what I can do with Ames and Hall in the meantime. Tell Boyle when we know more."

She bit down on her lip as her gaze swept the room, probably remembering the last time she had been in this room at night, and he thought she was going to say no. His gut clenched. Then she said, "Okay, tonight," and everything inside him leaped as much as it had when they'd made the breakthrough on the case just moments earlier. He cursed under his breath. Seemed working on Ames and Hall wasn't the only work he needed to do today—he also needed to shut his body into lockdown before Lucy knocked on his door again.

* * *

When he opened the door to Lucy that evening, there was an awful formality between them. Only his son seemed to make her relax. Josh squealed from his place on the lounge and reached his arms out, and Hayden felt a stab of envy—he wanted to hold his arms out to Lucy, too.

As he watched her with Josh—both of them talking and laughing—he couldn't tear his gaze away.

Then Hayden's cell rang and he was almost relieved by the distraction. When he picked it up, the number that flashed on the screen was unfamiliar.

"Hayden Black," he said.

"Mr. Black, this is Rowena Tate. I'm Senator Tate's daughter."

The senator had mentioned today that his daughter was in town, but Hayden hadn't met her, so the call was something of a surprise. "Good evening, Ms. Tate."

"I've been following the congressional committee's investigation," Rowena said. "As you know, my fiancé has an interest in the proceedings."

The senator had also mentioned Rowena's engagement to Colin Middlebury, a British diplomat who'd worked with Senator Tate to have Congress ratify a privacy treaty, and had helped the senator form the committee looking into the phone hacking in the first place.

"What can I do for you?" he asked as he tracked Lucy's progress across to his kitchenette to get a glass of water, Josh on her hip.

"I have a suspicion about one of the key players at ANS that you might be interested in."

His attention snapped back to the phone in his hand. "I'm listening."

"Any chance you can meet me tonight at the airport? I'm flying back to L.A. in a couple of hours."

"Tonight?" he repeated, wrapping a hand around the back of his neck. It was almost Josh's bedtime and he hated the idea of dragging a sleepy boy out in the dark of night. "Tonight might be difficult."

Lucy moved into his field of vision. "If you have to go out," she whispered, "I can stay with Josh."

"Hang on a minute, Rowena," he said, not taking his gaze from Lucy. Then he put his hand over the receiver. "I can't ask you to do that."

"Is it about the investigation?"

"Yes."

"I'm helping you with the investigation," she said, sweeping an arm toward the piles of documents they'd been sorting through. "Staying with Josh is simply part of that."

"But it's his bedtime in about an hour."

"He's had dinner, hasn't he?"

"Yes," he said, running a finger around the inside collar of his shirt, "but—"

"I'll handle the rest. I've helped out at my charity enough to handle one bedtime. You can show me where things are before you go. We'll be fine."

He glanced down at his son—who was gazing adoringly at Lucy—wondering if a good father would leave his son with someone else this way. His gaze flicked back to Lucy. He might not trust her about Graham, but he trusted her implicitly with his son. "Are you sure?"

"One hundred percent." She nodded decisively. "Go."

"Thanks," he said, then removed his hand from the phone to speak to Rowena. "I'll be there."

Six

Hayden scanned the crowd in the airport terminal until he caught sight of Colin Middlebury in a café. He headed over and held out his hand. Colin and the woman at his side pushed their chairs back and stood.

"Thanks for coming, Black," Colin said, shaking Hayden's extended hand.

"Good to see you again, Middlebury." He'd met the British diplomat when he'd first taken on this job, but hadn't met Rowena before.

"This is my fiancée, Rowena Tate." Colin put an arm around Rowena's shoulders and beamed at her.

The willowy blonde smiled first at the man beside her, then across at Hayden. "Thanks for coming on such short notice."

"It's no problem," Hayden said, trying not to think about Lucy looking luscious on the sofa back at his hotel suite.

Colin indicated a third chair at their table, and they all sat, both men turning to Rowena and waiting.

"We won't take much of your time, Mr. Black. I asked you to come because I didn't want to discuss this over the phone, given the nature of the investigation."

"Sensible." He knew his cell was safe from hacking, but he couldn't be sure about anyone else's. He glanced around—no one was sitting close enough to overhear. "So what's your suspicion?"

"It has to do with Angelica Pierce." She leaned closer over the table, and lowered her voice. "She's always seemed oddly familiar, but I saw her on the TV reporting a story and the camera caught her at an unusual angle, just off to the side. And I was suddenly struck by her similarity to a girl I went to boarding school with, Madeline Burch. Different-colored hair and eyes, and, if it's her, she's had a nose job and some other work. While she was still on the screen, I called a friend who went to Woodlawn Academy with us, and she thinks it could be Madeline, too."

Interest piqued, Hayden took a small notebook out of his shirt pocket and wrote the name Madeleine Burch. "Any reason a reporter changing her name to something more appealing is suspicious?"

"Madeline was...*unbalanced* is probably the best word. Always bragging that her father was someone big, but she never said who. Apparently he'd paid her mother some hush money so they couldn't mention his name. And if anyone challenged her on it, she'd lose it."

"Define *lose it,*" he said, suddenly very interested.

"One time she'd had argument with another girl. I can't remember what it was over. And that night when we went back to our rooms, the other girl's clothes were all over the floor, cut into pieces."

He arched an eyebrow. "Anything done about it?"

"They had no evidence." Rowena shrugged one shoulder in a gesture of helpless frustration. "Madeline told the teachers she saw a younger girl sneak into the dorm room, which was a lie. That girl wouldn't have hurt a mouse."

He rubbed his chin as he considered the woman before him. Rowena was showing no signs of lying—she seemed confident and open. On the current evidence, he was inclined to believe her.

"Was that an isolated incident?" he asked, taking notes on what she'd said so far.

"Unfortunately, no. She was unpredictable and vindictive. And even though we always knew it was her, she'd try to blame her crimes on someone else. Even conning younger girls to confess a couple of times. We pretty much gave her a wide berth whenever we could. Until the day she was arguing with another student about her 'secret father' and the other student called her a liar and a freak. Madeline attacked the girl and was finally expelled."

His pulse picked up speed as bits of information fitted together like interlocking puzzle pieces. "Did you see her again?"

She shook her head. "When all this came up recently, my friend Cara Summers and I searched the internet and couldn't find a trace of Madeline after she was expelled. And, oddly enough, Angelica Pierce doesn't have much of a trail before then. I'm not sure if it will help, but I decided it was better to tell you than not."

He nodded at the couple, his poker face in place despite the way his mind was racing. "I'm glad you did."

Rowena handed over an envelope. "These are the results of our research, such as it is. Mainly basic information, and we suspect that much of it is falsified. I'm sure you have other channels to go deeper. But there is one photo of Madeline that Cara managed to track down from another old school friend." Hayden thanked both Rowena and Colin, said goodbye and made his way out through the airport. If Angelica was Madeline Burch, she could have set up Troy Hall and Brandon Ames to carry out the plan then take the fall—that would fit the pattern of Madeline's school days. His blood pumped faster as his investigator's senses twitched. Something about this felt *right*.

Variations of possible scenarios played out in his mind on the trip back to the hotel and, as he used his key card to open the door, he was still buzzing with the new directions his investigation could take. This was a lead that could break the case wide open and point the way to solid answers.

Everything in the suite was silent, so he quietly walked behind the sofas to peek into Josh's room. His little boy was sleeping peacefully. Relieved, Hayden smiled as he shut the door. He'd have to thank Lucy later—

Then he saw her curled up asleep on the sofa and his breath stilled. Despite the temperature-controlled room, his skin heated.

She was so achingly beautiful, with her blond hair falling over the creamy curve of her cheek. Memories of touching her bare skin assaulted his senses, of the fragrance of her hair, the shape of her hip. Of her fingers touching him, feather-soft at first, then urgently when she needed him. Without realizing he'd moved, he was beside her, crouching down, close enough to feel her breath fan gently over his face.

His heart frantically battered at his rib cage, and a distant part of his brain screamed to move away before she woke, but he didn't pull back. Couldn't. He swallowed hard. Her skin was porcelain smooth, her lips slightly parted as she dreamed. Would he be in those dreams? She'd certainly been in his.

He leaned forward just a few inches and kissed her lightly. Sweet torture. His eyes drifted closed. He'd pull back any second now. He would. Just as soon as he committed this moment to memory.

With the softest of moans, Lucy moved her lips languorously under his and her eyes fluttered open. Now was the time to move away, *now,* but she smiled against his mouth and threaded her fingers through his hair and he couldn't summon the will to allow any space between them.

"Hayden," she murmured, then kissed him again. As she lifted herself up on an elbow, he slid an arm around her, dragging her against his chest, silently cursing the fabric between them. He was lost, drowning in her. The musky scent of warm skin surrounded him, curled through his mind, luring him to the edge of sanity, to a place where the reasons this was wrong didn't exist.

Yet a tendril of awareness remained, a slow-blinking warning light in the peripheries of his mind. He tried to push it away, to give himself over completely to the lushness of the woman in his arms, but deep down he knew…

Thrusting a hand up to cradle the back of her head, he kissed her one more time, a kiss tinged with desperation, before wrenching his mouth away and sitting back on his heels.

"Lucy," he said, his voice barely audible through a tight jaw. "I'm at breaking point." He dropped his forehead to rest on hers, holding her more tightly. "I want you—I can't tell you how much I want you—but making love again would be wrong on so many levels."

She pulled back and moistened her lips, unknowingly daring him to throw caution to the wind again. She blinked up at him, as if she was only now truly waking up, then she relaxed and smiled sleepily. "It'll be fine. Come down here. After last time I know there's enough room for two."

Frustration clawing through his veins, he speared the fingers of both hands through his hair, then tangled them together behind his head. "There's nothing I want more in this moment, but you know we can't."

She pushed herself up to a sitting position and rubbed her eyes. The movement just made him want to draw her into his arms even more, so he forced himself to go over to the other sofa, creating something of a safety barrier. Though if her pink tongue peeked out and wet her lips one more damn time, that distance would provide no obstacle at all.

She tucked her legs up beneath her and nodded. "Okay. Let me make a proposal."

"Sure," he said. It would need to involve a suit of body armor for one of them if it had any chance of effectiveness. Or perhaps separate cities.

"Here's how things stand." She held up a closed hand, ticking the points off by raising a finger for each one as she went. "We have some undeniable chemistry. You're only in D.C. for a short time. You don't have space in your life for a relationship. Your work won't allow for a relationship with me in particular."

He winced. Said aloud like that, their situation sounded even more hopeless than it did in his head. But he nodded slowly, prepared to hear her out. "I'm with you so far."

"Then we'll have a secret fling," she said, smiling, seeming pleased with herself.

Everything inside him tightened, ready to accept her offer, but he frowned. "What is that? Just sleeping together?"

"Purely physical," she confirmed. "Completely under the radar."

Was she serious? His body might already be on board, but the idea was insane. However, Lucy didn't seem to be joking. "The investigation—"

"We're both already compromised—this will hardly make it worse. Tell me," she said, tucking strands of blond hair behind her ear, "has sleeping with me convinced you of Graham's innocence?"

"No." Graham was guilty, he had no doubt, and nothing but irrefutable evidence to the contrary would change his mind about that.

She tilted her head in acknowledgment of his point. "Are you at all likely to alter your findings because of our intimacy?"

"Not a chance." It was inconceivable that he'd ever alter his findings. Integrity was everything in this business, to say nothing of his own sense of right and wrong.

"Then we're good," she said and nodded. "We can have a fling."

"A fling," he repeated. He really didn't have enough blood in his brain for this conversation. It had all headed south at the first touch of her lips, and now he was struggling to follow Lucy's reasoning.

"It solves everything. It's a great plan," she said, holding upturned palms out as if this was obvious.

He stood and stalked to the window, hoping the movement and view of nighttime D.C. would bring clarity. It didn't.

"You're okay with this?" he finally said. "A purely physical arrangement." He might want her more than he wanted any woman, but he wouldn't use her. It went against everything inside him.

Her blond brows drew together and she glanced down at her hands, as if deciding how much to confide. "I don't want anything serious right now. You say that your focus is on your son and your business—well, my focus is on my career." She paused and the skin around her eyes pulled taut. "Because of who my father and stepfather are, I have to work twice as hard as anyone else to prove my independence, prove myself. And to be honest, after the work I've already put in, the last thing I need is a relationship with a rich older man who has a high profile and connections."

He drew in a long breath, suddenly struck by her meaning. He'd been worried about his reasons for not getting involved, but hadn't thought about it from her side before. She had as much to lose as he did. Yet she still wanted him enough to propose this plan.

He crossed to the sofa she was perched on and sat on the armrest, taking her hands in his. "We'll have an affair with an end date of when I leave town, both of us going in with our eyes open." He managed to keep his voice even, but his entire body was straining forward at the thought.

"So you want to?" she asked, her voice surprisingly uncertain.

"Lucy, I want to more than I can say. But I have conditions." He released her hands and stood again before he consigned his own conditions to hell and took her there on the sofa. "First, we keep the rule we already made about secrecy. No one can know we're doing this. And the rule about us not letting our involvement influence us."

"Done," she said simply.

An electric shiver raced down his spine. This was really going to happen. He cleared his throat before continuing. "Also, no making love here in my suite. It's the center of my investigation, I keep research here and I meet people here. We only sleep together at your place, and only during the day when Josh is with his nanny. The geographical distinction will keep a firm boundary in our minds so we don't compromise the investigation."

GET 2 BOOKS

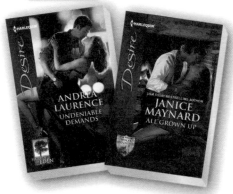

We'd like to send you two *Harlequin® Desire®* novels absolutely free. Accepting them puts you under no obligation to purchase any more books.

HOW TO GET YOUR
2 FREE BOOKS AND 2 FREE GIFTS

1. Return the reply card today, and we'll send you two *Harlequin Desire* novels, absolutely free! We'll even pay the postage!

2. Accepting free books places you under no obligation to buy anything, ever. Whatever you decide, the free books and gifts are yours to keep, free!

3. We hope that after receiving your free books you'll want to remain a subscriber, but the choice is yours– to continue or cancel, any time at all!

EXTRA BONUS

You'll also get two free mystery gifts!
(worth about $10)

FREE!

Return this card today to get
2 FREE BOOKS and 2 FREE GIFTS!

HHARLEQUIN®

YES! Please send me 2 FREE *Harlequin® Desire®*
novels, and 2 FREE mystery gifts as well. I understand
I am under no obligation to purchase anything, as
explained on the back of this insert.

225/326 HDL FVQ9

Please Print

FIRST NAME

LAST NAME

ADDRESS

APT.#

CITY

STATE/PROV.

ZIP/POSTAL CODE

Visit us at:
www.ReaderService.com

◀ DETACH AND MAIL CARD TODAY! ▼

❤HARLEQUIN® READER SERVICE— Here's how it works:

Accepting your 2 free books and 2 free mystery gifts (mystery gifts worth approximately $10.00) places you under no obligation to buy anything. You may keep the books and gifts and return the shipping statement marked "cancel". If you do not cancel, about a month later we'll send you 6 additional books and bill you just $4.55 each in the U.S. or $4.99 each in Canada. That is a savings of at least 13% off the cover price. It's quite a bargain! Shipping and handling is just 50¢ per book in the U.S. and 75¢ per book in Canada.* You may cancel at any time, but if you choose to continue, every month we'll send you 6 more books, which you may either purchase at the discount price or return to us and cancel your subscription.

*Terms and prices subject to change without notice. Prices do not include applicable taxes. Sales tax applicable in N.Y. Canadian residents will be charged applicable taxes. Offer not valid in Quebec. All orders are subject to credit approval. Credit or debit balances in a customer's account(s) may be offset by any other outstanding balance owed by or to the customer. Books received may not be as shown. Please allow 4 to 6 weeks for delivery. Offer valid while quantities last.

If offer card is missing, write to: Harlequin Reader Service, P.O. Box 1867, Buffalo, NY 14240-1867 or visit www.ReaderService.com

BUSINESS REPLY MAIL
FIRST-CLASS MAIL   PERMIT NO. 717   BUFFALO, NY

POSTAGE WILL BE PAID BY ADDRESSEE

HARLEQUIN READER SERVICE
PO BOX 1867
BUFFALO NY 14240-9952

NO POSTAGE
NECESSARY
IF MAILED
IN THE
UNITED STATES

"Makes sense," she said, her face serious but voice breathless. "I'm good with that one."

He knelt down in front of her, wanting there to be no misunderstandings on the next point. "And if it becomes awkward or too much for you, promise me you'll say so."

Nodding, she laid her hands on either side of his face. "I'll promise, if you will."

"Sure," he said, barely able to form the word when she was so close and touching him.

"I can work from home tomorrow."

Blood sparking as if it carried an electric current, he mentally ran through his schedule. "I don't have any appointments in the morning. I'll be over at nine-thirty." She moistened her lips and he groaned. "Though if you don't leave this second, we'll start right this minute."

With a look of mischief, she grabbed her bag and practically scurried out the door, and Hayden was left alone and wondering how he'd make it till nine-thirty.

At ten past nine, Hayden answered a knock at his hotel-suite door. The only appointment he had this morning was to see Lucy in twenty minutes…to begin their fling. His skin heated. He'd been dressed and ready for the day—for Lucy—since eight. The nanny had come for Josh at nine, and for ten minutes Hayden had been restlessly shuffling papers, willing the hands on his watch to move faster.

When he pulled the door open, Angelica Pierce stood there in a figure-hugging red dress, pulling her Botoxed lips into a plastic smile. "Hayden, darling," she said brightly.

"Good morning, Angelica." His training came to his aid, allowing him to smile and be pleasant without betraying either his annoyance at being delayed from seeing Lucy or his increased suspicions about Angelica after meeting Rowena last night. "Did we have an appointment?"

"No, no," she said as she brushed past him and into the room. "I was in the area and I thought I'd touch base. See if there's anything I can do to help."

"You want to help?" he asked mildly, digging his hands into his pockets.

"Of course I do! These awful crimes tar all journalists with the same brush in the public's mind. The sooner it's all cleared up, the better for news broadcasters everywhere." She sat on the sofa and patted the cushion beside her. "Come and sit next to me, Hayden, so we can talk about it."

The sight of Angelica on the sofa where he'd kissed Lucy less than twelve hours ago was jarring. "I'm sorry, but I need to leave for a meeting."

"Oh, *darling,* I think you'll make time for me." She stretched her neck to one side and lowered her shoulder, and the sleeve of her blouse fell down her arm, revealing a perfectly tan shoulder, unencumbered by a bra strap.

Despite his urge to throw her out, Hayden regarded her pose analytically. It was a clear invitation, and from what he knew of Angelica already, if he handled this badly she might overreact. And if she did, that might make her slip up and reveal something…

"Angelica," he said, finding a polite but firm tone. "I really do have to leave."

She pushed herself up from the sofa and slinked over to his side, standing too close. His skin crawled. When he stepped away to create a little distance, she followed.

"Hayden, let's not waste words." Her smile was part sex kitten, part great white shark. "I know you're interested in me, and I'm attracted to you, too."

"Angelica," he said bluntly, crossing his arms over his chest. "It's not going to happen. Not now, not ever."

There was silence for a long beat. Then, as if a switch had been flicked, she roughly grabbed her sleeve and tugged it up, her aqua eyes sparking with rage.

"This is because of *her,* isn't it?" A finger with a fire-engine-red nail jabbed the air in the direction of the door.

Hayden stilled. "Who?"

"Lucy Royall," she spat with more venom than a rattlesnake. "She was all you wanted to talk about the other day. You have a little crush on her, don't you?"

A trickle of unease seeped down his spine. He'd thought she'd turn her anger on him, not Lucy. Had he put Lucy in the line of fire?

Angelica must have seen something on his face that gave him away, because she smiled, satisfied.

"Don't worry, darling, all the men do. It's the princess act she's perfected. But let me give you a friendly word of advice." She paused, a devilish gleam in her eyes. "Your little crush is doing an investigation into you. Gathering material for an exposé that will air soon on ANS. I heard it directly from Graham Boyle last night."

An icy hand crept over his heart and squeezed. Lucy had played him? Was working on an exposé when she'd told him she wanted to help his own investigation? No, he refused to believe she could be that manipulative. Although…how well did he really know her? Nausea roiled in his stomach, leaving a bitter taste in his mouth. Maybe she was capable of planning this. And, if so, was her idea of a *fling* all part of the scheme?

Whatever was going on, he wasn't sharing a thing with the woman in front of him. "I think it's time you left, Angelica," he said and strode over to the door.

"Sure." She'd morphed again—this time into a sincere

confidante. "When you're ready to talk, let me know. I'm the one who can help you, remember that. And in the meantime," she said, slinging her bag over her shoulder and heading out the door, "don't give that Royall actress anything you don't want to see on prime-time news."

Three minutes later, Hayden was in the rental car on his way to Lucy's place. This morning's visit might have been planned as a romantic liaison, but now they'd use the time for Lucy to give him some information. The truth would be a good place to start.

Seven

It was almost ten o'clock when Lucy saw Hayden's car pull up. With butterflies in her belly, she looked down at her soft cream wraparound dress—easy to remove—which covered lacy lavender lingerie. The ensemble had seemed appropriate for the start of a fling, though she'd changed outfits twice already, and had been having second thoughts about this one for about ten minutes. If he hadn't arrived now, she would have darted back upstairs and changed again.

Pulse jittery, she opened the door to him. "You're late, Mr. Black," she said in her best saucy voice, then registered his thunderous expression. Her heart skipped a beat. "What's wrong?"

He pushed past her, strode into her living room, then turned to face her with hands low on his hips. "You're doing an exposé on me?"

All the air rushed from her lungs. "How do you know?" she asked in a raspy whisper.

"Rules about secrecy, rules about a fling." His coffee-brown eyes flashed fire. "One we forgot to add was a rule about not gathering material for an exposé while we were *sleeping* together."

Her knees wobbled, but she stepped forward. "Hayden—"

Ignoring her attempt to explain, he walked across the room and leaned a hand over the window frame, looking down on the small courtyard at the back. "At least I was up-front about my investigation. You knew what I was doing from the start, and I told you I suspected Graham and that you were covering for him." He swiveled to face her again, eyes narrowed. "Apparently I don't deserve the same courtesy."

"Okay, you're angry," she said, slowly crossing the room toward him. "I get that. And I'll allow that you have a right to be."

He coughed out an incredulous laugh. "Generous of you."

"But your investigation could ruin a man's life. An innocent man." Her stepfather, who'd been nothing but kind and generous to her for ten years. "Graham could lose his company, his reputation, even his freedom. And there are people in ANS who would set him up to ensure that happens. You don't think we'd have a plan B in this situation?"

"That Boyle and ANS would have a plan? Sure. That you'd be leading it?" He ran a hand through his hair, his gaze pinning her to the spot. "It's a rotten way to treat a man you're sleeping with, Lucy."

"You're right. I'm sorry." She sank down into the overstuffed sofa and pulled a cushion into her lap, suddenly bone-weary from all the different directions she was being pulled. "But you have to understand that when Graham asked me to do the piece, I'd only met you once. I didn't know if I could trust you."

He held up a hand. "Do you trust me now?"

"Yes." She sighed. "I'm not sure when that happened, but I do."

"So why not tell me yesterday? Last week? After we slept together?"

It was a fair question, one she'd been asking herself. "I guess I was hoping you'd uncover the ringleader of the phone hacking and your investigation would be over before the exposé was ever needed."

"And what if the timing didn't work like that, if I took longer?" He paced across the room, then turned on a heel to face her again. "Were you going to tell me before the show aired? Or let me find out along with everyone else?"

"I would have warned you, I swear. And for what it's worth, I'm sorry, Hayden. But put yourself in my shoes for a moment. My boss—my stepfather, a man I love— tells me to work on a secret project that could save him. I only met you a few weeks ago. Are you saying I should just switch my loyalties like changing socks?"

He winced as the point hit home. "You were stuck between your family and your lover."

Her shoulders dropped a fraction of an inch. "This thing between us is crossing boundaries left and right, isn't it?"

Hayden blew out a breath, seeming to deflate somewhat, and came over to sit on the coffee table in front of her, their knees brushing. "Yeah, it is. I've been thinking I should hand the case to someone else in the company."

"No," she said, grabbing his hands. "Please don't."

He tilted his head to the side. "But I think Graham is guilty. It could be better for you to try your luck with someone else."

"You might think he's guilty, but you're honest and honorable. As soon as we find the evidence that exonerates Graham, you'll respect that. You're our best hope, Hayden." Every word she'd said was true, but there was something else, something even stronger pulling at her insides, demanding she not let him go. Not yet. *Please, not yet.*

He looked at her for a long moment and she held her breath, waiting for his decision. Finally, he nodded once and relief flooded her veins. Even as she smiled her gratitude and released the tight grip she had on his hands, somewhere in the back of her mind was a niggling voice saying her reaction was too strong for simply having an investigator stay on the case, but she brushed it aside.

Hayden rubbed a palm over his closely shaved jaw. "You said before that people in ANS are setting him up. Why would you think that?"

This was better—stick to the investigation and Graham. Safer. She rose and padded on bare feet across the carpets to the kitchen, filled two glasses with sparkling water and handed one to Hayden. When she saw him leaning against the island counter, her mouth dried. His dark, masculine beauty was emphasized by the pale marble countertops and white cupboards. She didn't tend to have people at her place very often—she usually met friends out—so Graham was the only person who'd spent much time in her kitchen. Maybe if she'd had more men here, she wouldn't feel so overwhelmed by Hayden's presence. He wouldn't seem to dominate it so much. But she doubted it—that was Hayden's effect wherever he was.

She took a sip of the sparkling water to moisten her throat so she could speak. "You said yourself that someone was pulling the strings. Whoever that is, they don't plan on going down for this. Passing the buck up the ladder is the perfect alibi." She took another sip, thinking back over the clues they had, then stilled. "Who told you about the exposé?"

"Angelica," he said, distaste clear in his voice. "She just came to my room, tried to seduce me then gave me a friendly warning not to trust you."

Lucy's heart skipped a beat at the *tried to seduce me* comment, but she managed not to let her personal reaction affect her professional interest in the development. "It's Angelica behind this whole thing. I know it is."

"I think you're probably right." He put his empty glass in the sink, then leaned back against the counter again.

I think you're probably right? Had he seen the truth? "So you think Graham is innocent."

"No," he said, shaking his head. "He still must have known what was going on, perhaps worked with her on it, but I suspect Angelica masterminded it."

She crossed her arms under her breasts. "You'll see about Graham. By the end of the investigation, we'll have the evidence that he's innocent." Graham's nature was to push as far as he could go, but once he hit the edge of legality, he'd stop. He wasn't the first man to believe in an employee who turned out to be bad.

"Listen," he said taking her hand and interlacing their fingers. "Something else about Angelica's announcement bothered me."

"The attempted-seduction part?" She grinned, inordinately pleased at the thought of Hayden rebuffing another woman's advances.

He shook his head as if that was inconsequential. "No, that was easy to fend off. It was the venom she has for you. She didn't even try to hide it."

"She's always hated me." Lucy shrugged. It was something she'd accepted within a week of joining ANS. Angelica treated everyone below her badly and seemed to take special pleasure in targeting the boss's stepdaughter. She wasn't the only one—Marnie and Mitch had been the same way. Par for the course with a last name like Royall and a stepfather who owned the network.

Hayden tugged her closer with their joined hands. "This was something beyond hate. Way beyond."

His gaze was intent, and this wasn't a man who spooked easily. She swallowed. "Oh."

"Why would she hate you specifically?" He traced a pattern over her hands with his thumbs. "You've never had a run-in?"

"I don't know. I always thought it was because I was the stepdaughter of the network's owner. They resent having me in their workspace."

"Could be. But why is she more vindictive than the others? And if she's capable of manipulating at least two people in a complicated scheme of illegal phone hacking— and having them cover for her even after their arrests— then she's not a person to underestimate."

"She wouldn't do anything to me," Lucy said, but even to her own ears her voice sounded unconvinced.

"Lucy, this is my area of expertise. Angelica Pierce would hurt you if she got the chance. I want you to stay close to me, where I can protect you. Tell ANS that you need to stick near me while you're working on the damn exposé."

Something inside her chilled. Angelica would hurt her if she had the chance? What sort of person operated that way? She'd known about Angelica's complete lack of ethics in her reporting and information gathering, but this was something else altogether....

She withdrew her hands from Hayden's clasp and wrapped them around her waist. Journalism had once seemed a shining light of truth-seeking and integrity. Seeing the tape of Troy Hall and Brandon Ames hiring hackers to illegally invade people's privacy hadn't affected her too much, because she'd figured the pair were rogue elements. But Angelica Pierce was a star reporter, and even though Lucy had known she was nasty, before she'd worked at ANS she'd idolized Angelica's reporting. What was the saying about never meeting your idols…?

She lifted her chin. One thing was for sure—Angelica wouldn't get the better of her. "I'm not a child in need of protection. I'll be fine."

"Believe me, I know you're not a child." He ran his fingers down her arm and then drew her against him. "Let me protect you," he murmured in her ear.

At every point of contact, her skin heated until champagne sparkles fizzed through her bloodstream. But she tried not to lose herself in her body's reaction to him.

"It's not your job," she said against the cotton shirt covering his chest.

He smoothed fingertips down her sides till he reached the curve of her hips and drew her even closer. "I want to protect you. I want you safe."

She winced. The last thing she needed in her older lover was for him to think of her as a damsel who needed rescuing—couldn't he see that?

Laying her palms flat on his chest, she eased away so she could see his eyes, so he could understand this was important to her. "Hayden, I don't want you to see me as someone you need to look after."

His gaze softened, then blazed. "There are many things I see in you. Your courage and determination. Your lush curves. That someone who's possibly crazy has it in for you. That I can't stop thinking about making love to you again. That—"

"Stop there." She moistened her lips. "Go back to that one."

"That someone who's possibly crazy has it in for you?" he drawled with a knowing smile.

She shimmied against him. "The one after that."

He lifted her hand to his lips and kissed one fingertip after the other. "I can't stop thinking about making love to you again?"

Her breath caught high in her throat. "That's the one. Tell me more about that."

"There are the waking thoughts and the dreams at night," he said, turning them so she was trapped between his solid body and the counter behind her.

"Start with the dreams."

He gave her a slow, sensual smile full of promise. "In my favorite one, I was in bed at home in New York, and you slipped through the door and climbed under the covers with me."

She shivered as the image formed in her mind. "What was I wearing in this dream?"

"Nothing." His voice dropped to a seductive whisper. "That's why it's one of my favorites."

Her eyes drifted closed and a dull throb pulsated at her core. "What happened once I was under the covers with you?"

His freshly shaved jaw scraped over her cheek as he pressed his lips to her ear. "I spent the rest of the night making sure you had a good time."

Her heart skipped a beat. "And did I?"

"Oh, yes," he said, teeth nipping at the side of her throat. "You were very enthusiastic in your appreciation. When I woke, I was surprised you weren't still there."

Such a simple fantasy, but it aroused her to the tips of

her tingling toes—thinking about what they'd done, but also just that Hayden Black had dreamed about her.

She wound her arms around his neck. "Sounds like a dream that was meant to come true."

"I'm working on it." He glanced around. "You got a bedroom in this place?"

"Down the hall. Tell me about the waking thoughts," she said, and bit down on her lip.

He swung her up into his arms and headed out of the room. "They mainly center on regrets."

"Regrets?" She placed a hand on the side of his face, bringing his gaze back to her as he carried her along the hall. "About making love to me?"

"Yep. I've got a list." He indicated the open door to her bedroom with a tilt of his head and she nodded.

"Such as?"

"It happened too fast," he murmured in her ear, his mouth hot. "I didn't get to do some things I wanted."

He eased her down on the pale blue coverlet, then climbed onto the bed, prowling over her, filling her vision. "To taste the skin just where your diamond pendant hides." Slowly, he undid the tie holding her wraparound dress together and pulled it open. She held her breath as one hand firmly cupped the lavender lace he'd uncovered and his head dipped to the hollow between her breasts. The heat of his mouth and tongue sent a shower of sparks through her bloodstream, and when his teeth gently bit at the slope of her breast she arched up, offering more, wanting more.

When he lifted his head, his eyes were as dark as night, and filled with banked desire. "Or to feel the satin smoothness of your inner thigh," he said as a hand snaked down her body and drew one knee up. He kissed a trail down her belly, around her hip, to her leg and up to her raised knee while his fingertips traced circles on her inner thigh near the edge of her panties.

"I didn't get to linger in places I wanted to." His tongue joined his fingers and she came close to dissolving on the spot. "I'm a man who hates having regrets, so if it's all the same to you, I'll be rectifying the situation right now."

"Be my guest," she said breathlessly.

For what seemed like hours, Hayden drove her slowly out of her mind, bringing her close to the edge then ruthlessly turning his attention to yet another sweet zone, removing pieces of clothing as he went. All the while, she explored the ridges of his abdomen, the powerful muscles of his shoulders and arms, the rough hair covering his thighs, every part of him she could reach, peeling his clothes away until there were no barriers between their skin except the protection. They didn't have forever, she knew that, but for now he belonged to her. Today and for a few days she laid claim to his body; here in her bed, his attention was focused on her. And there wasn't another place in the world she'd rather be in this moment. Maybe there never would be again.

Hayden paused, looking deep into her eyes, then his lips came down to meet hers, all his passion and hunger coalescing into one perfect kiss. She practically floated off the bed, but Hayden's weight pressing down on her kept her anchored.

"Lucy," he rasped when he broke away. "I've never wanted anyone this much." He shook his head, as if having trouble believing it himself. *"Anyone."*

He lifted her knee and, without losing eye contact, entered her. Air hissed out from between his clenched teeth, and, unable to restrain herself, she called his name. His eyes flared and he began to move, slowly at first, then faster. She arched her back, wanting everything he could give her, wishing this could last forever, needing him more than she'd thought possible. When she reached the edge, he captured her mouth, pushing her right over the brink, not slowing, keeping her soaring high, then followed, her name wrenched from his throat. As she drifted back to earth, Hayden eased up, then pulled her along the length of his body. She'd never felt as safe, as cherished. Never felt as much herself. Would anything—any man—be enough again?

Later that afternoon, Lucy sat in Graham's office, a large lump of panting bulldog at her feet. She fingered the framed photo still sitting in a box on her lap, surrounded by tissue paper—her fifteen-year-old self, standing between Graham and her mother, beamed up at her. Her stepfather had arranged for it to be reproduced and framed and had given it to her when she'd walked in a few minutes ago.

"Thank you for this," she said through a ball of emotion in her throat.

"I know you still miss her." His voice sounded a little affected, as well.

She touched a fingertip to her mother's face in the photo. "I do." Graham gave her presents regularly, but this one was priceless.

"So how's the research for the exposé going?" he asked as he leaned back in his chair, changing the subject as he always did once it became too emotional. "We almost ready to start production?"

She tucked her hair behind her ears in an effort to stop a guilty blush from creeping up her cheeks. "Not so much."

"You haven't found anything?" Deep frown lines appeared across his forehead.

A barrage of images filled her mind of all the things she

had found out about Hayden Black—the ridges of muscle that crossed his abdomen, the way the dark hairs covering his chest felt against her cheek, the expression on his face when he found release inside her....

She picked at a spot of lint on her skirt, then shrugged a shoulder. "There don't seem to be any skeletons in his closet. He's a good man, a newly single parent and straight up and down in his job." Her research had found evidence of minor issues, such as an uncomfortable relationship with his deceased wife's parents, and some hard partying when he was a student, but nothing that would fill an exposé. It wasn't even worth mentioning now.

Graham waved her assessment away with a sharp slashing motion. "There must be something you can find."

"Actually, I've hit a slight snag." She rubbed Rosie's chest with the toe of her shoe as she formed the question she needed to ask. "How far do you trust Angelica Pierce?"

Graham didn't hesitate. "Good journalist. Solid instincts."

"She told Hayden that I was doing an exposé on him."

His eyes widened. "Damn."

"I thought you didn't trust anyone else to know that plan." That was the part that had surprised her the most about the whole situation.

"She came to me last night, worried about what damage Black's investigation might do to the network. I told her we had it covered. I was going to use her to front the piece, so she would have found out soon enough anyway." He picked up a pen and began tapping a furious beat on his desk. "She went straight to Black?"

Straight to him with the information, plus a bonus attempted seduction. "She dropped in on him this morning."

"She must've thought she could use it to get some leverage. Get him to back off, or give up his sources."

Lucy bit down on her lip, amazed he was already explaining away Angelica's actions. Making excuses for her. Couldn't he see what was under his nose?

"Until this is over," she said carefully, "I don't think you should trust her."

"Rubbish. Angelica won't bite the hand that feeds her. She'll put ANS's interests first." He threw the pen he'd been tapping across the desk and scrounged in a drawer till he found his ever-present antacid tablets. "How did Black take the news? Is he going to be difficult?"

Given the things Hayden's mouth had done to her this morning, she'd say he'd taken the news very well, all things considered. "No, he'll still let me help with his investigation. I convinced him I'd be ethical about it."

Graham grinned as if he thought she'd lied to Hayden, and something inside her withered. Angelica's ruthlessness had given Lucy pause. But Graham seemed to respect that about his star journalist. And now he'd shown approval at the possibility his own stepdaughter would lie and double-cross someone. She'd known Graham was a hard-nosed businessman, but she'd—probably naively—thought that there were different expectations of the journalists at ANS.

Where did that leave her plans for her own career? If she refused to be like them, to play in a sandbox with loose rules, did she have a future in broadcast journalism? Her stomach hollowed out. She had no answers.

"I need to get back to Hayden," she said, reaching for her hold-all bag and pushing up out of her chair. "I said I'd help him with some research this afternoon."

Graham's brow folded into deep wrinkles, making him resemble Rosie. "You're not getting too close to Black, are you? Don't be fooled into sympathizing with your target. Rookie mistake."

She thought of Hayden stretched naked across her sheets only a few hours ago, smiling lazily at her as she brought them a tray with toast and coffee.

Her hand fluttered up to circle her throat. "No, we're not too close."

"Good," he said with a decisive nod. "I knew I could count on you."

But Lucy had begun to wonder—just who really could count on her? And just as important, who could she count on? She looked down at the photo of her with Graham and her mother for long moments, then slipped it into her red bag. She rolled her shoulders back and pushed the disloyal thoughts away. Graham could count on her and she could count on him. They were family.

She gave Rosie a final scratch under the chin, hugged Graham quickly and left.

Hayden stared at the two photos side by side on his laptop screen, a triumphant rush filling his veins. The resemblance was unmistakable. Without taking his eyes from the computer, he reached for his cell and dialed Lucy's number.

"Can you come over?" he asked when she answered. They'd fallen into a routine over the past few days of taking personal time at her house each day—but at varying times, for discretion's sake—and her dropping over to his hotel either in the afternoon or evening to touch base on the investigation. But now it was only 7:00 a.m.; Lucy would be on her way to ANS soon and his discovery couldn't wait a full day.

She didn't hesitate. "Sure. What's up?"

Unwilling to say too much on the phone, he simply said, "I've found some things you'll want to see."

"I'll be there as soon as I can."

By the time Lucy arrived, Hayden had put together a slideshow of the images his office had sent him and strapped Josh into his high chair for breakfast. As he opened the door, he stole one lingering kiss, then before he drowned in her floral scent and broke their rules by dragging her off to his bed, he led her over to share his discovery.

"What have you got?" she asked, her hazel eyes bright with curiosity. She kissed Josh on the top of his head and slipped into the chair Hayden had pulled over on the other side of his, laying a hand proprietarily over his thigh. At the simple gesture, something moved in his chest.

He froze. This was supposed to be a fling—was he becoming emotionally entangled? No, he wouldn't let himself. There was no future for a single father from New York with a twenty-two-year-old heiress from D.C. Ignoring her hand and any deeper implications it represented, he turned the laptop screen so she could see the images and gave Josh a spoonful of stewed fruit.

"After a bit of digging, I found a photo of a girl called Madeline Burch." He clicked the mouse and a picture of a teenager with mousy brown hair, plain features and dishwater-brown eyes appeared. "When I met with Rowena Tate that night at the airport, she said that she and a friend had suspicions about Madeline Burch. She gave me a photo of Madeline from their school days, but the resolution was too low. So I found a better one and sent it to the tech guys at my office. They did some imaging work and came up with these projections."

He gave Josh another spoonful with one hand and clicked the mouse with the other. The same girl now appeared with straight blond hair. On the next click, she had aqua-blue irises. Then lips that were plumper.

"If Madeline colored her hair, wore contacts, had her lips done and had a nose job—" he clicked the mouse again and the same girl now had a different nose "—then she becomes more recognizable."

"Angelica," Lucy murmured. She took the baby spoon from him and stood, seamlessly taking over feeding Josh while watching the screen over his shoulder.

"Bingo. Angelica Pierce started life as Madeline Burch. I've also tracked Madeline's records, and she disappears a couple of years after graduation. Angelica's records go back to school years, but the tech guys in the office looked deeper and found they're all plants. She's tried to cover her tracks, and it's worked, to an extent."

Lucy tapped a fingernail against the bowl she held. "That's a pretty thorough makeover."

"No doubt about it." He flicked through the slideshow again as he spoke. "My main question now is, did she do this for a new start, maybe to increase her chances of scoring an on-camera job…"

"Or is she hiding something?" Lucy finished for him.

He nodded. "I've made a few calls, and no one from her school has stayed in contact with Madeline. She was brought up by a single mother who's passed on, and doesn't seem to have any other family. Several women remember that Madeline was always bragging about having a rich father whom she couldn't or wouldn't name, but other than that, no one knew much. I had my staff trace her birth certificate, but her father wasn't named."

"And I'm betting we won't be able to find anyone who knew Angelica Pierce as a child."

"Not that I've found so far." He flicked his pen over and under his fingers as his mind ticked through the facts.

"In fact, besides you, I can't find a single person who will say a bad word against Angelica. Troy Hall and Brandon Ames will only sing her praises, even though I'm pretty sure she set them up."

When Josh finished eating the stewed fruit, Hayden wiped his face with the washcloth and Lucy took the bowl to the sink.

"She's got to be blackmailing them with something," she said over her shoulder.

"Agreed." He unbuckled a clapping Josh and lifted him free of the high chair before giving him a quick hug and depositing him on the sofa with his toys. "If she's gone to this much trouble to reinvent herself, I can't see her setting someone up and leaving a loose thread. She would have had the blackmail material before choosing Ames and Hall to take the fall."

"You know," she said slowly, as if she was uncomfortable with what she was saying. "I talked to my stepfather and mentioned that Angelica had told you about the exposé. But he still trusts her."

Hayden scanned her face, looking for signs that there were layers to what she was saying, but couldn't find any. She was honestly telling him that she was surprised Graham Boyle still trusted Angelica Pierce after Angelica had betrayed him. It hit him then that Lucy truly believed her stepfather was innocent. She wasn't covering for him—she really had no idea that Boyle was behind the illegal activities at ANS. Anger simmered that Boyle could have someone with a pure heart like Lucy in his life and risk dragging her into his sordid work. He should have kept Lucy away from ANS, away from a company that would likely leave her tarnished. Lucy deserved better.

He sank back into his chair at the desk. If he shared his thoughts with her, she wouldn't believe him. She'd continue defending Boyle with more loyalty than the creep deserved, so instead he simply said, "Angelica's ability to make people trust her is what's gotten her this far."

She reached into her hold-all bag and came out with a pale yellow muffin. She broke a large chunk off and handed it to him. "Lemon and poppy seed. I bought it on the way over."

He took the chunk and bit in as he looked back at the images on his laptop. Angelica seemed to be holding all the cards. Everything came down to her, but they didn't have one shred of evidence. Yet.

Brushing her hands, Lucy turned to him. "So what do we do next? We can't just wait for her to slip up."

"I'm heading to Fields, Montana. The president's birthplace is where this whole debacle started, and I'd lay down money that it's where Angelica started her hacking on this story. If I can get the evidence that she did, I can catch her." Fields had been the place where Ted Morrow had gotten Eleanor Albert pregnant, the place from which Eleanor and their baby, Ariella, had disappeared. Journalists had been crawling over the town since Morrow declared his bid for the presidency, and since the story about Ariella Winthrop had broken, investigators and police had joined in, and their discovery of phone taps had sparked the congressional investigation. But they had focused on Ted Morrow's and Eleanor Albert's friends and families. Hayden had been through all that evidence and one thing still bugged him—why were all the hackers looking for a baby in the first place?

In the video that captured Hall and Ames hiring the hackers, they'd specifically asked for confirmation there had been a baby. What had sparked the idea to search for that? And who had found those first glimmers of the story? It was time to widen the circle of his investigation to cover more residents of Fields. Lucy's overheard conversation about Nancy Marlin, friends of Barbara Jessup, was his strongest lead, and the place he'd start.

"How long will you be gone?" Lucy asked.

"A couple of days." Which was a couple of days too many to leave Lucy alone in D.C. unprotected. He'd been serious about Angelica being a potential threat, and he wasn't willing to take a single chance. He cupped her shoulders with his hands and found her gaze. "Come with me."

Eight

Lucy looked at Hayden, her head and heart at war. Now that he'd shared her bed, a couple of days apart seemed an eternity, so going with him to Montana was tempting on that factor alone. But there were unspoken words in his tone that made her think there was something else behind the invitation.

She stood to give herself some distance and took a few steps away. "Why do you want me to come?"

"We've been working together, so it makes sense." He casually shrugged his broad shoulders and leaned back in his chair. "Can you get the time away from work?"

She was sure she could, since Graham wanted her to focus on the exposé, so the more time with Hayden, the better. Still, Hayden's expression was too serious, too concerned.

"A few days ago you were angry at me for not being honest about doing the exposé. You said you'd been upfront. So, do it again now—be straight with me." She crossed her arms under her breasts. "Why do you want me to come to Montana?"

He pushed his chair away from the desk and stood, but he didn't come closer, as if respecting the distance she needed for this conversation. "I don't want to leave you in the same town as Angelica when I'm not around. I don't trust her, and she's fixated on you."

"I'd been in the same town as Angelica for years before you came along."

He shook his head. "That was before. Her visit here a few days ago showed she's on edge. She knows the walls are closing in."

"You think you need to protect me," she said, voice flat.

"Of course I should protect you." He rubbed the back of his neck. "It's my investigation that's pushed her. It's my responsibility to make sure you're safe."

Responsibility? There was that word again. Her stomach hollowed out. The last thing she wanted her lover to see when he looked at her was someone to be responsible for. Would he think that if they didn't have a ten-year age difference? Would he see a woman his own age as able to look after herself?

She straightened her spine. "I can take care of myself."

"I know you can, Lucy. But if I'm right about Angelica, she's capable of things worse than we already suspect her of." With hands around her shoulders, he pulled her close and whispered in her ear. "Did I mention Josh will be staying in D.C. with the nanny? And that I'd book two suites in a new spa hotel—one for us and one for appearances. The one for us would have a hot tub built for two." He placed several damp kisses on the shell of her ear, then pulled her lobe into his mouth, making her blood sizzle.

"Hayden…" she said on a sigh as she melted into him.

"I could make you very glad you agreed to come."

Oh, yes, she knew he could. That fact wasn't in question. What she needed to decide was whether she *should* go. Hayden's hands slipped down to her waist and, nudging the edge of her blouse up, found bare skin just above her skirt. The delicious heat started to rise, and all reservations about going away with him evaporated.

"Okay," she said, swaying against him. "But no more telling me what you think I want to hear. Promise you'll just say what you mean."

"Promise." His lips moved across her cheek and captured hers in a kiss that was as much a vow as his word had been.

As the check-in receptionist at the Fields Chalet handed over the keys to her suite, Lucy smiled and thanked him, then moved aside so Hayden could check in to his suite. A buzz of excitement had been building deep in her belly since they'd left D.C. On the flight, and at both airports, she and Hayden had acted as if they had only a professional relationship, a charade they were keeping up for now.

She glanced around the foyer, all thick wooden poles and soaring glass panes showing the spectacular mountain view beyond. She'd been to Fields to ski in the past, but had always stayed in her aunt's villa on the mountainside, which was kept fully stocked, so she hadn't strayed into town. Since Hayden needed to interview people in the old township, they'd booked into this high-end chalet on the main street. Its grand opulence could have seemed out of place a few doors down from the feed store and across the road from a sawdust-and-peanut-shells tavern, but the chalet had landscaped the area between the road and the front door to create a buffer between the two worlds of Fields.

In the years the president had gone to school here, it

had been a sleepy town of ranching families and local businesses, but over time that had changed. The rest of the country, including Lucy's own aunt Judith, had discovered the stunning skiing and snowboarding location and development had soon followed. Now Fields was a hybrid of the charming old town and shiny new developments.

Hayden came up behind her and she could feel the warmth emanating from his body. Not touching him during the trip had been a special kind of torture.

"Would you like me to help you to your room?" he asked politely, taking her carry-on suitcase.

"Thank you," she said in the calmest voice she could muster. "That's very kind."

They set off for the elevators, her body vibrating with the need to feel his skin under her fingertips, his mouth on hers. Hayden hit the button for the elevator, and in the partly secluded alcove, he dared to let the desire in his gaze flare to life.

"I hope you don't have plans once you reach your room, Ms. Royall," he said, his voice low.

A shiver raced across her skin. "Something in mind?"

"Hell, yes," he said as the doors whooshed open.

As soon as they'd entered and the doors closed out the world, she turned to him. "Hayden—"

Before she could get any other words out, he'd pushed her against the wall, his hips pressed against hers, and claimed her mouth. Everything inside her melted and she dropped her handbag to the floor so she could use her hands to touch him—shoulders, biceps, neck, wherever she could reach. Under her fingers, his body shuddered, which only made her belly tighten even more, made her want him more. She arched her back, bringing her hips into closer contact with his, and was just considering pulling his shirt from his trousers when a chirpy bell sounded and the doors opened.

Hayden groaned as he pulled away. "I couldn't wait another second." He thrust a hand in front of the closing door to keep it waiting for them. "That trip was far too long—being so close, but not being able to kiss you."

She swallowed, trying to get her voice to work. "And now there's the walk from this elevator to our rooms. Yours or mine?"

"Your room, my room, I don't care." He cupped her chin and gave her bottom lip a butterfly-light caress with his thumb. "As long as it's a room with a bed."

She trembled with anticipation. "Then my vote is for the closest one."

The corner of his mouth quirked. "Race you."

He stepped out of the elevator, holding the doors open until she'd picked up her handbag and followed, then he strode down the hall, carrying both the bags, faster than her legs could keep up with. She caught him as he stopped to open the door with the key card. He grabbed her around the waist, pulling her through the door with him and nudging his carry-on bag through with a shoe.

The heavy door shut behind them and she had a few seconds' glimpse of the opulent room with a gas fireplace and a majestic view of the mountain before Hayden dropped her bag and took up their kiss where they'd left off in the elevator. This time she wasn't wasting any time and, as his tongue moved in her mouth, she undid his belt and slid it out of the loops on his trousers before throwing it as far across the room as she could.

When she reached for his zipper, Hayden pulled her hands back and wrenched her shirt over her head. "I need to feel your skin, to taste it." His mouth came down on her shoulder, his tongue moving, teeth scraping across to her collarbone.

She moaned and felt for the wall behind her, taking a small step back, using it to help her stay upright. Hayden followed, pinning her against the cool wall as he found her mouth again. She pulled his shirt from his trousers as she'd wanted to do in the elevator, and he broke away for the seconds it took to grab it from the back and yank it over his head. When he came back to her, the feel of his bare chest on her sensitized skin made a sob rise in her throat. The dark, crisp hair brushed against her cheek while she tried to catch her breath, the muscles moving under her fingers as he kept moving, unzipping his trousers and kicking them away, divesting himself of his boxers, then sliding her skirt up her thighs and moving on to her panties.

"Condom?" she asked with what was probably her only remaining brain cell.

He held a foil packet up between his fingers. "I threw a couple in my pocket in case of an emergency."

"This certainly qualifies as an emergency," she said and took it from him, ripped it open and rolled it down his length, luxuriating in the solid feel of him.

The instant she was finished, he lifted her and brought her legs around his waist. She pushed against the wall at her back to give her traction and slid down onto him, all the breath leaving her body in a ragged sigh as she did.

He stilled and looked at her with such hunger, such raw need, that her pulse spiked even higher. "You know there's a bed about ten feet away," she whispered.

"Too far," he said as he moved inside her, and all thought stopped. All she could do was feel—feel his hot mouth on her throat, the building wave inside, the frantic need that grew with every touch, every movement, until it was too big to contain and it reared up and crashed down over her, through her, and she was helpless to do anything but hold on to Hayden with every last bit of strength she had. Within moments, he rasped her name and shuddered, and she gripped him even tighter, panting, never wanting to let him go. Never.

Never.

Her skin turned cold. *Never?* This was a fling. Of limited duration and purely physical. She unwound her legs and slid down his body, and let him lead her over to the bed. Had she left her heart unguarded? Hayden pulled her down and under the covers, then wrapped her in his arms. Squeezing her eyes tight, she ignored the fluttering in her belly and let herself enjoy him for the time she had left. She'd deal with the fallout of a bruised heart when—*if*—it happened.

A couple of hours later, Hayden pulled the rental car up in front of a little cottage with bright pots of flowers and plants clustered on the porch and the paved walkway that led from the front gate. A little painted sign on the mailbox proclaiming "Jessup" showed they'd found the house of the former maid to the president's family. His gut told him this was where Angelica Pierce's phone-hacking odyssey had begun.

Lucy undid her seat belt and turned to him. "What are we looking for?"

Hayden straightened his tie, reconsidering the wisdom of bringing Lucy. His main thoughts had been about getting her out of D.C. while he was away, and keeping her safe from Angelica, but when he'd been trying to convince her to come, he'd implied she'd be helping with the investigation. Unfortunately, he hadn't thought much past her safety till this morning.

"Hayden?"

"Tell me I'll be able to trust you in there," he said gruffly.

Her cheeks flushed pink. "You're doubting me?"

"I'm acknowledging your split loyalties."

"I've already proved you can trust me several times, including not telling Graham about Nancy Marlin when you asked me not to." Her gaze was unwavering. "I'm on the side of truth, Hayden."

His shoulders relaxed a fraction as he accepted her words. "Okay. But just so we're clear, this interview is confidential."

"Not a problem. I'm actually looking forward to seeing you interview someone else."

"I usually run interviews alone, but if you have something to ask, let me know."

"Which one am I—good cop or bad cop?" Her eyes twinkled with humor and suddenly he had to clench his hands on the wheel to stop himself reaching for her and feeling that curving mouth under his own.

"Barbara Jessup hasn't done anything wrong, so we can probably dispense with the bad-cop role this time. Though if you're still in the role-playing mood when we get back to the chalet—"

She laughed as she opened her door and said over her shoulder, "Let's just deal with this meeting first."

Barbara Jessup was an older woman with neatly pinned-back white hair and a welcoming smile. Hayden made the introductions when she met them at the door, and explained that Lucy was an ANS employee who was working as a consultant on this case. When she brought them into her living room, there was a plate of homemade cookies and a pot each of coffee and tea. He'd already spoken to her on the phone and she'd been keen to help, so after only a few minutes of small talk, they were able to jump to the heart of the matter.

Hayden placed his small recorder on the table and turned it on, then picked up his notebook and pen. "You spoke to Angelica Pierce, a journalist at ANS?"

"Oh, yes. A couple of times. The first time was back when President Morrow was just a senator. I always knew that boy would go far," she said, pride filling her features.

"Then you spoke to her again more recently?"

Barbara picked up the plate of cookies and offered them around as she spoke. "About the time he was elected. Ms. Pierce said she had a few more questions."

Hayden took a raisin-and-nut cookie but put it on his plate, keeping his hands free for taking notes. "Did you tell her about Eleanor Albert and the baby?"

The older woman squirmed a little in her seat. "In the first interview, she was asking about his school days and his friends, wanting to know if there were any left living here she could talk to. I gave her a few names, and when we came to dear Eleanor, I said I didn't know where she was now and hadn't seen her since she moved towns after giving up her baby."

Just as he'd suspected, Angelica had stumbled over the information that had started the story. "Did you mention the baby might be the president's?"

"Of course not!" Her teacup clattered into its saucer. "I'd never betray the family that way, even if I did know the truth."

"I'm sure they appreciate that," he said with a genuine smile. He liked Barbara Jessup. "When Angelica Pierce came the second time, did she ask about the baby again?"

Barbara sniffed. "She certainly did. But I told her I didn't know anything."

"And did you know more than you told her?"

"I know a lot of things about a lot of people, including about that baby. That doesn't mean I'll tell a journalist." She looked pointedly at Lucy.

Lucy's brows drew together and Hayden smothered a smile. "As I said, Lucy is helping with this investigation—you can trust her. Do you have friends or family who know the same things about Eleanor and the baby as you? People you might have talked to on the phone after Angelica left?"

Her face crinkled up in thought for a moment. "I did phone my friend Nancy Marlin and told her how the interview went."

"Nancy knew about the baby?" He'd been planning to ask about Nancy Marlin since Lucy had overheard Angelica and Marnie discussing her, but it was even better that it had arisen naturally in the conversation.

"She worked for the Morrows for one summer, the one when Eleanor left, so she knew—or suspected—as much as me."

He caught Lucy's gaze. There was a faint flicker in her eyes that most people would have missed, but he'd come to be able to read Lucy—her investigator's senses had perked up the same time his had.

He looked back to Barbara Jessup and gave her a warm smile. "This is very important, Mrs. Jessup. Think back to that phone call for me. Did either one of you mention in that conversation that you thought the baby might have been Ted Morrow's?"

Her hand flew to cover her mouth, her eyes wide. "Is it all my fault?" she said from between her fingers. "Has that boy got all this trouble falling on his head because of me? I wasn't even sure the baby was his. Oh, sweet Jesus, what have I done?"

Lucy moved over to the sofa beside Barbara and put a comforting hand on her arm. "No, Mrs. Jessup. This is not your fault. You did really well when you were interviewed. You kept the Morrows' secrets."

He'd bet money that after Ted Morrow was elected president, Angelica, like hundreds of other journalists across the country, had gone looking for a new angle. Something different to put on TV. She would have gone back over the footage and interviews from her first trip to Fields, looking for tidbits. When she saw the baby mentioned again, she would have done a simple internet search, as Hayden had done, and found Eleanor Albert was Ted Morrow's prom date. There was no record of Eleanor Albert having a baby, or even of Eleanor herself after high school, so Angelica would have had no idea if she'd gotten pregnant within a time frame that could implicate the president.

So, hoping for a scoop, she would have gone back to Fields, interviewed the same people again, stirred up memories, and planted the taps on the phones. She'd lucked out when she overheard Barbara and her friend Nancy discuss the baby and their theory that Ted Morrow had been the father. Then she would have had Ames and Hall hire the hackers that focused on Ted Morrow's and Eleanor Albert's friends and families—the infamous scene that had been caught on tape—and they found enough information to run the story that had aired after the president's inauguration. It was all clicking into place.

"I'm sorry to tell you, Mrs. Jessup," Hayden said as gently as he could, "it's very likely there's a tap on your phone and some of the conversations you thought were private have been overheard."

Her face twisted in disgust. "That's plain wrong, that's what that is."

Lucy's gaze met his again, just briefly, but in that moment he knew their thoughts were completely in sync. He felt somehow warmer.

"We agree," he said, nodding. "And I'll be working hard to make sure those responsible face justice. In the meantime, I can take care of your phone for you. And if you give me a list of your friends Angelica or her team spoke to, I can check their phones, as well."

"You're a good man, Mr. Black." She turned to Lucy and patted her hand. "You hold on to this one real tight."

Lucy's mouth opened, startled. Hayden hesitated with his coffee mug halfway to his mouth. If Barbara Jessup had suspected their connection, they'd have to be more careful of betraying it, become more circumspect when they were together.

And even if he could admit there was something between him and Lucy, neither of them would be holding on to the other one tight. What they had was temporary. Physical and temporary.

Before Lucy could reply, Hayden stood and headed for the phone in the corner of the room. "I'll start with this one."

They stopped at a deli in town for lunch after their interview with Barbara Jessup. While Hayden waited for their sandwiches to be made, Lucy found a pretty table on the sidewalk. The town had an interesting vibe with the mix of traditional and new and she soon lost herself to people watching—a lifelong pastime that came in handy now that she was a journalist on the lookout for stories.

"Lucy? Is that you?"

She twisted in her seat to see her aunt—a tall woman dressed in understated elegance—emerging from the ski shop next door. Within moments, Lucy was off her feet and finding herself wrapped in a warm embrace.

"Aunt Judith," Lucy said, hugging her tightly.

Judith stepped back, pulling a tissue from her bag and

dabbing at her eyes. "I didn't know you were in Fields, sweetie. You should have let me know."

Lucy felt her own eyes mist over and blinked the moisture away. She should make more of an effort to see her father's family—a couple of times a year was nowhere near enough. Being busy might be true, and it definitely had been easier to spend time with them when her father was alive and able to be the conduit, but family was important.

"I'm here for work," she said, promising herself she'd visit again, soon. "Otherwise I absolutely would have called."

Judith's face brightened. "How long?"

"Just tonight."

"You'll have to come up to the villa for dinner."

She glanced back to the deli, where Hayden was waiting for their order. "I'm traveling with a colleague."

"Bring them," Judith said with a generous sweep of her arms. "Philip and Rose are here, too, so we'll make a cozy group."

From the corner of her eye, she saw Hayden approaching their table. How would he react to the invitation? He'd made his feelings about his ex-wife's family clear— inherited money didn't impress him. In fact, he'd been disdainful of their lavish lifestyle. Aunt Judith was her father's sister—a Royall through and through—and had expensive tastes to go along with her wealth.

She stepped away from her aunt and turned to Hayden, who'd placed the sandwiches and drinks on the table. "Judith, this is Hayden Black. Hayden, this is my aunt, Judith Royall-Jones."

Hayden reached out a hand. "A pleasure to meet you."

"And you, Mr. Black. I was just telling Lucy to bring you up for dinner tonight at the villa."

Hayden turned to her and raised an eyebrow. She started to shake her head, wanting to save him from a situation he might find uncomfortable.

"We don't get to see enough of our Lucy, so I won't take no for an answer." Judith linked her elbow though Lucy's and grinned, obviously certain of Hayden's answer.

He looked from her aunt back to her, then a charming smile spread across his face. "In that case, I'd love to come."

Nine

That night, Hayden drove the rental car up the mountainside to Lucy's aunt's lodge. They'd spent the afternoon visiting Barbara Jessup's friends whom Angelica had interviewed and checking the phones at each house. Most had taps. There were a few more people he wanted to interview in the morning, then he and Lucy would catch a lunchtime flight back to D.C. But before that, there was dinner with some of Lucy's family to contend with.

He cast a quick glance over to the passenger seat. Lucy was staring out the window, seemingly lost in thought.

"So who will be there tonight?" he asked.

She turned to him, tucking a few strands of shiny blond hair behind one ear. "Aunt Judith and Uncle Piers—it's their lodge. My cousin Philip and his wife, Rose. She didn't mention anyone else, but with Judith, nothing surprises me." She reached over and laid a hand on his thigh. "Hayden, I'm sorry you were dragged into this."

"It's no trouble. Besides, maybe I'd like to meet some of your family." It was true—his curiosity was piqued about the Royalls. During his marriage, he'd thought Brooke's family wealth had been the cause of her pampered-princess ways. But Lucy's family was much richer than Brooke's, and Lucy hadn't shown a sign of the high-and-mighty or petulant behavior that Brooke had wielded like a weapon. Lucy had obviously been raised very differently.

He covered her hand on his thigh with his palm. "But if you're really sorry, how about you make it up to me later?"

She laughed. "Deal."

Lucy directed him to the house and when he turned into the drive, he gave a low whistle. "When you said lodge, I was expecting, I don't know, a lodge. Not a mansion." The place was huge—four stories built into the side of the mountain so each level was stepped in as it went up. Glass and wood everywhere, a soft golden glow coming from many windows, and a carpet of spring flowers that wove around paths. It looked like it belonged in some kind of fairy tale.

"Aunt Judith likes her little comforts," Lucy said with an ironic twist to her mouth.

He chuckled. Going by what he could see of the house, that was something of an understatement.

Judith met them at the door, taking Lucy's hands and squeezing. "Lucy, dear. I can't tell you how thrilled I was to see you in town today."

"Me, too," Lucy said with genuine warmth.

"And Mr. Black." She turned a welcoming smile to him. "I'm glad you could come."

He shook her hand. She was tall, with glossy silver hair that came to just under her chin and hazel eyes that reminded him of Lucy's. He liked her already. "Call me Hayden."

"Then you must call me Judith. Please, come in."

She led them through a house that was all soaring glass and warm wood tones. Fires crackled in grates as they went past, and thick wall-to-wall carpets kept the rooms toasty from the spring-night air in the mountains.

They emerged from a hallway into a large library with soft yellow walls, fresh flowers on small tables and built-in bookshelves on each wall. Three people were already standing in the room, each holding a sparkling crystal glass—he recognized them from Lucy's descriptions as Piers, Philip and Rose. Piers and Philip came over to give Lucy hugs, and Judith performed the introductions.

Within minutes, Hayden had a martini in his hand and was ensconced in small talk with Philip that mainly revolved around skiing and red wine. Every so often he met Lucy's eyes across the room and lost his place in the conversation, but he seemed to cover well enough for Philip not to notice.

Partway through a discussion on the finer points of choosing a good merlot, Judith interrupted them to lead the group into the dining room—a room with spectacular views of the town below. Hayden found himself seated with Lucy on one side and Rose on the other and served stuffed mushrooms that appeared to be a traditional family favorite. The main course followed and conversation flowed smoothly among the group.

"So, Hayden," Judith said in a deceptively sweet voice once the plates were cleared. "Are you married? Single?"

Hayden cleared his throat. "Widowed."

"Oh, I'm sorry to hear that." Judith's tone was sympathetic, but she clearly intended to pursue the topic. He shifted in his chair and prepared to redirect the conversation.

"Hayden has a little boy," Lucy said from beside him.

He held back a smile—she'd dived in to protect him from her family. She was a good woman, that Lucy.

"How old is he?" Judith asked.

Hayden took a sip of his wine. "He just turned one."

"Such a lovely age," Judith said. "I remember when Philip was that little. He was so sweet, always rushing up with flowers he'd picked for me."

Hayden saw Philip look across the table at Lucy and share a glance of amused exasperation. Either not noticing or not minding, Judith continued. "And Philip was always being carried around by one of his sisters when he was one. He milked it for all he was worth."

"Smart boy," Hayden said to Philip and grinned.

Philip tilted his head in acknowledgment. "What's your boy's name?"

"Joshua. Josh." His chest hurt, missing his little boy—he hadn't been away from him overnight since Brooke died and he'd taken complete parental responsibility. He was already looking forward to seeing him again the next afternoon.

Judith leaned forward. "Do you have a photo of him?"

Hayden found one in his wallet and passed it across to Rose, sitting to his side, just indulging in a quick look himself first. "It's a couple of months old now, but he looks much the same. Just bigger."

"He's gorgeous," Rose said, and passed the photo along the table. Hayden's chest expanded an inch or two. Josh was the best son a man could hope for.

"So you'll be on the lookout for a new mother for him?" Judith asked, smiling to cover for her complete lack of tact.

"Mom," Philip interjected good-naturedly. "The man lost his wife not long ago. Give him a little peace."

"It's okay," Hayden said. "It has only been three months, but, no, I won't be looking for a new mother. I won't marry again." He resisted the impulse to glance over at Lucy and gauge her reaction, but she'd known their relationship was only temporary. This shouldn't be too big a shock for her.

"Maybe with time…" Judith began but let her words trail off when Hayden shook his head.

"It's not about time, or healing. It's about parenting. This might sound selfish, but I'm not prepared to share decision making about Josh ever again."

Judith's brows shot up with unbridled interest. "You didn't agree with your wife's philosophy on child raising?"

"Not even close to agreeing with it," Hayden said with blunt honesty, which seemed to please Judith. "In fact, I was locked out of most of the decisions. Obviously, I should have challenged it at the time, but I didn't. I won't risk a situation where I don't have a say about my own son again."

"What about love?" Judith asked, leaning back in her chair, wineglass in hand. "You can't control that."

"Love isn't the most important thing. Josh is," Hayden said. There was nothing he was more certain about in his life. "I know I'm not a perfect father. I'm still learning as I go, but I have a clear vision of what I want for him, and I won't compromise. Even for someone I loved."

"Aunt Judith," Lucy said, "I was thinking I might show Hayden your garden before dessert. Even at night, it's gorgeous. Besides, I think Hayden's put up with enough of the Royall inquisition for one night."

The others laughed, including Judith. "Go ahead," she said, waving an arm in the direction of the door.

"C'mon," Lucy whispered.

Hayden followed her down a hallway into a small room full of boots, coats and paraphernalia, glad for the chance to be alone with her for a few minutes. Her family seemed nice enough, but he'd choose time with Lucy outside in the dark without question.

She took two coats down from hooks and handed him one. "It's quite cool at night."

He held her coat for her to thread her arms through, then pulled the larger one on before following her outside. The landscaped side yard was terraced and bursting full of spring flowers, most of which had closed their buds for the night, yet still looked magical in the moonlight.

"I'm sorry about Judith's questioning," Lucy said as they walked along a winding paved pathway. "She means well, but she's used to being the matriarch and pretty much being able to do and say as she pleases."

He found her hand and intertwined their fingers, loving the slide of her skin against his. "I didn't mind. She reminds me of my mother. A bit nosy, but good people."

They walked farther along, then Lucy stopped and pointed up to the sky. "There's the moon. I wonder if it's waxing or waning—living in the city I lose track."

"It's nice," he whispered. "But it's not the prettiest thing out here." Cupping her cheek in his palm, he brushed a thumb over her lip. She was so beautiful. Incandescent. And when she looked at him with those hazel eyes filled with rich desire for him, he was lost. He dipped his head and found her mouth, waiting and ready for him. With excruciating patience—he couldn't afford to get carried away in her aunt's garden—he kissed her, just lightly, a gentle sweep across that landed at the corner of her mouth, a hint of teeth as he nibbled on her lush bottom lip. She shuddered and moved in closer. Her lips were beguilingly soft as they moved beneath his, but still he held himself in check. Then she sighed and her tongue slid against his and suddenly the kiss was carnal and he was helpless to pull it back. He tightened his hold on her and she pushed her hands under his coat, to move across his chest.

They were seconds away from being completely undone, so he wrenched his mouth away but stood, chest heaving, for long minutes before he could get his throat to work.

"Lucy," he finally said. "Unless you're ready to go back to the chalet right now, we need to stop doing that."

"You're right." She squeezed her eyes shut, but didn't let her hold on him loosen.

"And if we go inside now, with the way you look, all rosy cheeks and puffed lips, they'll have no trouble guessing what we've been doing." He said the words calmly enough, but he hated the need for secrecy. If he could walk back into that room and have everyone know he'd kissed Lucy senseless out in the moonlight, he'd be the proudest man in the state. She was the sort of woman a man was proud to have by his side. Instead, they had this mess of rules and secrets that sat more uncomfortably inside him each day. He rubbed a hand through his hair. "How about we talk for a couple of minutes? Till we lose that just-kissed look."

She dug her hands deep in the pockets of the coat and looked up at him. "You really believe what you said to Judith about not sharing Josh again? That you'll always be a single father to him?"

"I do." He'd given it a lot of thought over the past three months. It was the best arrangement for everyone, no question.

"That's kinda sad," she said softly. "I don't want to think about you being alone for the rest of your life."

Her sympathy didn't sit well. This was his choice and he was happy with it. "It's not the rest of my life. Only until Josh is older. And I wouldn't always be alone. Just never married again."

She looked out at the view of the town below. "That's still sad."

With a finger, he turned her face back to him. "You only think it's sad because you have such a good heart."

"You have a good heart, too," she said, but there seemed to be more behind her words. Was she having second thoughts about ending their arrangement? Perhaps this sympathy was Lucy's way of telling him he didn't have to be alone, that she wanted things to continue. His chest constricted painfully. He couldn't let her start thinking that way, let her be set up for disappointment.

"Maybe once I had a good heart," he said carefully, needing her to understand this. "But it's jaded now. Yours is fresh and pure—" he laid a hand over her chest and could feel her heartbeat "—far too pure to be polluted by someone like me. I hate to admit it, but the sooner I'm out of your life, the better for you. Though I can't deny I'll miss you like crazy once I'm gone."

"I'll miss you, too." She drew in a long breath. "Maybe if I'm up in New York—"

"No." Though he flinched as he said it. "The cleaner the cut, the better. Remember our rules? No emotional entanglement, just physical. If we let it linger, it'll turn into something neither of us wanted. Something that might become bitter, and I don't want anything to tarnish the memories I'm taking of you."

"I'll cherish these memories forever," she said, and he could see her eyes glistening in the moonlight.

Unable to help himself, he kissed her again, pulling her flush along his body in the moonlight, wanting to create as many memories as he could before the inevitable moment their time expired.

* * *

Lucy and Judith carried the dessert plates into the kitchen an hour later. "Thank you for inviting us. It's been lovely to see you."

Judith pulled her into a hug. "I wish we saw you more." After long moments, she released her and began piling the plates up. "Shame that man of yours is so dead set against marriage."

"He's not my man," Lucy said and turned the tap on to rinse out the wineglasses.

"I've seen the way he looks at you. He's yours, even if it's just for now. Besides, you had no lipstick left when you came in from the garden."

Without thinking, Lucy touched two fingertips to her lips, then dropped them when she saw Judith's knowing smile. Lucy shut the tap off and leaned back on the bench to face her aunt. "It's temporary. Even if he was interested in anything longer term, with the way people treat me, the expectations they have of me because of Daddy and Graham, the last thing I need is an older man who's already well connected and wealthy. They'll think I've taken the easy route again, found someone to look after me."

"Maybe," Judith said and scraped some scraps into the bin. "But I like him."

"I like him, too." Lucy bit down on her bottom lip. It was the first time she'd admitted to herself or anyone that she really did like Hayden. Maybe she was even coming to love him. But defining her feelings was a pointless exercise—no matter how she felt, their fling would end soon.

Judith smiled at her. "The one thing I've learned over the years about relationships is that liking each other enough is all that matters." She tucked some of Lucy's hair behind her ear then rubbed her arm. "It's all that matters."

Lucy smiled back, but didn't reply. From where Judith stood—thirty-two years into a happy marriage with her college sweetheart—things might seem that simple. But for the rest of the world, relationships were complicated, messy things that sometimes had luck on their side and sometimes didn't.

Maybe if she'd met Hayden in ten years' time, things would have worked out better for them—she'd have already established herself, would know who she was without being surrounded by strong men, and Hayden would have an eleven-year-old son and be more relaxed about having a woman in his life. Their age difference might not matter so much if they were thirty-two and forty-two instead of twenty-two and thirty-two. But things were what they were, and wishing for them to be different wasn't going to help her when it was time for Hayden and Josh to leave D.C.

Four days later, with one arm around Lucy's waist, Hayden shut off the faucet in her bathroom's oversize shower with an elbow and slumped against the wall, chest heaving. They'd made love in her bed, then he'd suggested a shower before they both went to work, but seeing Lucy's water-slicked body had made the end result of that idea inevitable. It was probably a good thing their time together was only a fling—if this arrangement was permanent, it just might kill him.

Lucy looked up at him with a satisfied gaze. "Your imagination is a beautiful thing, Hayden Black."

"I aim to please," he said, grinning, and summoned the energy to step out of the shower. He passed a fluffy blue towel to Lucy, but regretted it when she patted herself down and wrapped it under her arms, tucking a corner in to keep it in place. He let out a resigned sigh. Damn shame to cover up a body like that.

She glanced over at him, one eyebrow arched. "Are you going to towel off, or are you trying the drip-dry method?"

"Just admiring the view," he said, then ran the towel over himself till he was dry enough. "What have you got today?"

She walked through the connecting door to her bedroom and pulled pure-white underwear from a drawer. "More research into your background. Graham is going to run the exposé next week, whether I've got enough material or not."

She dropped the towel and stepped into the white panties. Hayden swallowed. "Good luck."

The idea of the exposé airing didn't thrill him, but in his line of work, it was a cost of doing business. He had no deep, dark secrets, no skeletons in his closet. And if they made up stories, he'd deal with that when it happened.

"Give me some hints." She'd put on the white lace bra and was sitting on a velvet-covered stool at her dressing table, brushing out her damp hair. "Did you cheat on a high-school history exam? Were you involved in a street brawl?"

"Okay." The mirror on her dressing table showed another perspective of her movements, giving double the impact and mesmerizing him. "This is the one and only lead I'll give you. I organized a boycott of the school cafeteria when I was a junior."

Her eyes brightened and met his in the mirror. "A radical political statement? Please tell me you burned a flag."

"Eight kids got food poisoning in the same week and no one would look into it. We boycotted until the school board sent someone in. They fired a couple of staff who weren't following safety procedures and tightened up the practices."

"Yeah, that's just the kind of story we need," she said, throwing him an ironic smile over her shoulder. "You'll come off looking like a hero. Fighting for truth and justice since you were a kid." Her words might have been flip, but her eyes shone with pride, and it made his chest swell a little.

He grinned. "Take it or leave it."

"I'll take it. Maybe I can find a different angle." She crossed to her closet, took out a pale green blouse and slipped it on. "What are you doing today?"

He pulled on his trousers, then socks and shoes, giving himself a moment to decide how much to tell her. Lucy had proved herself trustworthy in this investigation several times, but this information was a whole new level—today he was going to a judge to get permission to perform surveillance on Angelica Pierce. The slightest slip to someone Lucy trusted, like Graham, who leaked it to Angelica, would make the whole exercise pointless.

She stepped into soft cream trousers and secured the buttons before resting her hands on her hips. "Some super-secret mission?" she teased.

He rubbed a hand across his jaw. "It might be better if I don't tell you."

"You're joking, right?" she said, her voice incredulous. "I've done everything you've asked of me, even not telling Graham about Angelica being Madeline Burch. Why wouldn't you trust me now?"

She was right, but this was different. "You've been great on this investigation. The difference is you're helping out to try and clear Graham's name. If it comes down to it, you'll choose Graham over any other option."

"Of course I'll stand by Graham," she said, her voice

carefully controlled. "He's innocent. Are you telling me you've got evidence on him?"

He shook his head, conceding her point. "No, but I don't think it will be long. And if you had to choose between the truth and your stepfather, where would you stand, Lucy?"

Eyes blazing, she seemed to grow about two inches. "You're questioning my personal integrity now?"

The accusation hit him square in the chest, but he didn't waver. "Most people have a line in the sand somewhere. Many don't know where that line is until they reach it."

"And you, the famous investigator—who even as a child stood up for truth and justice—do you have a line?" She stared at him, waiting while he didn't answer. Then, suddenly, her eyes softened. "Josh," she said.

He nodded, every muscle in his body tight. He'd let Josh spend his first nine months being raised Brooke's way, against his better judgment. Nothing, *nothing* was more important than Josh. And there was nothing he would choose over Josh's best interests ever again. Not a woman. Not his career. Not his own life. Josh was his line in the sand.

Lucy's line was Graham. And Graham was tangled up with Angelica, he had no doubt.

"Tell me honestly," he said, sinking down onto the side of her bed and resting his hands between his knees. "Let's say Graham had done something illegal, not phone hacking, some other crime, just to take it out of this context. Hypothetically, if Graham had done something illegal that had hurt someone else, would you turn him in?"

She frowned. "That's an impossible question. No one could answer that without knowing what the crime was."

"That's an answer in itself." Hedging her answer just

showed that there were crimes she would cover up for Boyle.

She crossed her arms under her breasts and tapped a foot on the carpet. "Then you answer a question for me."

"Sure."

"Is whatever you're doing today legal?"

"Of course it is," he said, taken aback at the question.

She waved away his implication of being affronted without pausing. "Is it ethical?"

"To me, without question." Everyone had their own ethics and principles, but he was pretty certain his plan would be within Lucy's framework of ethics, as well.

She sat down on the edge of the bed beside him. "Then tell me what it is and I swear I'll help you."

Hayden looked at her, weighing the options, then made his decision. He could use her help, and if she'd given him her word, he could trust her. "I'm getting an order from a judge to put Angelica under surveillance."

"That's it?" she asked skeptically.

"If this leaks back to her, say, via Boyle, the surveillance will be pointless, so I have to be extremely careful. But understand, I have the evidence to get the judge's order for Angelica. If I had evidence on Boyle, I'd get an order for him today, too."

"Key word there is *if. If* you had the evidence on him." She arched an eyebrow. "You don't have it because it doesn't exist."

"The surveillance on Angelica will flush something out on Boyle." Though he knew nothing would convince her until he uncovered the evidence. "You still willing to help?"

"You betcha," she said without hesitation. "I want to be

there when Angelica incriminates herself and whoever's been helping her."

"You and me both."

Ten

"Hi, Roger," Lucy said to the ANS night guard as she walked Hayden past the security desk over to the elevators. It was just after midnight, so, aside from the studios where the anchors reported the late-night news broadcast, the place would be relatively deserted. It was the only time Hayden would be able to put the wiretap on Angelica's phone. As soon as he'd been granted the court order, Hayden had brought some tech guys from his company down to do some more elaborate work on Angelica's phone lines, but he wanted nothing left to chance with this case, so that meant also planting a good, old-fashioned tap on the phone, as well.

The elevator doors closed and they were alone, except for the cameras she'd told Hayden about during the briefing in his hotel suite. Josh was back there asleep and the nanny was staying the night in Josh's room. A rush of nerves filled her stomach. This had to work—the surveillance had to find who Angelica was working with and clear Graham's name. She sent up a little prayer that they'd thought of everything in their preparations and this would all go off without a glitch.

"The weather was lovely today," she said, making small talk. Silence would look suspicious for the elevator cameras. If they were caught, Lucy would tell Graham that she'd played double agent—luring Hayden to the office so she could show him some of the information she'd uncovered, ostensibly helping him, but really hoping to see if his reactions pointed her to further discoveries to help her exposé. Did that mean she was a triple agent now?

"Sunny and warm, which was nice for Josh," Hayden said, as if discussing the weather in the ANS elevator was the most natural thing in the world. The man must have nerves of steel. Though he didn't have as much to lose as she did. For him, this was a case—albeit one he felt strongly about. For Lucy, her whole family was at stake. Graham was all she had.

The elevator arrived on the eighth floor, which housed most of the journalists, but the skeleton staff on the night shift all worked on other floors. Angelica's office was down at the end, alongside the offices of the other senior reporters, and Lucy had a desk in the cubicles in the middle of the open-plan room.

"This way," she said, guiding him along a single-file corridor made by glass office walls on one side and waist-high partitions on the other. The moonlight through all the glass in the offices meant there was little need for lights, which was lucky, since turning on lights would only attract more attention.

"Which desk is yours?" His voice was low and it sent shivers down her spine. Even with all she had at stake, sneaking through a darkened room with Hayden at her back, asking where she worked in a deep voice, was enough to distract her from their mission. She shook her head at herself, but led him to her desk anyway, then held an arm out as if showing him a million-dollar view.

"It's neater than the others," he said, turning to survey the surrounding desks quickly.

She glanced over the surface—everything in its place, from the pens in the penholder to the little stationery box that held anything else she needed. "I like to be organized."

He arched an eyebrow. "I'm organized, but my desk is messier than this."

"Your desk is neat," she pointed out. And the room in his hotel suite he'd been working from had been so neat, so devoid of personal effects, that she'd had trouble getting a sense of him when she first met him.

"It's not a real desk—it's just for interviews on this case. My desk in New York has haphazard piles of documents and trays filled with papers. The way desks are meant to be," he said, the corner of his mouth twitching.

She thought back to the mountain of baby manuals she'd seen in Josh's room, and the way he'd spread papers over the coffee table when she'd been there at night helping him research. Organized chaos matched his personality more than the tidy desk she'd been judging him by. It was as if she'd seen a little further into the man inside, the one he didn't show everyone, and it made her heart warm.

"So where is Angelica's office from here?" Hayden asked.

"Just there," she said pointing to the darkened room across the narrow corridor. "With the way my desk faces, I get to see her smiling face all day." Of course, Angelica took every opportunity to scowl at her, or to say something cutting when she walked past.

The elevator pinged and they both stilled. As the doors whooshed open, Angelica's sharp voice filled the air. "No, that's not acceptable. If you want a credit on the story, you'll have the research on my desk by 8:00 a.m. End of discussion." Then a beat later, as if talking to herself, "Moron." There was silence except for Angelica's staccato heels clicking on the tiled floor, coming their way.

Lucy looked at Hayden, her pulse jumping. It was one thing to be found by a random ANS staffer, or to have their escapade get back to Graham, but Angelica was a different story altogether. If she saw them, there was a good chance she'd suspect what they were doing and be on her guard, ruining the plan.

Hayden grabbed Lucy's arm, pulling her down to the floor and quietly squeezing them both under her desk. To fit in the small space, she was tucked into Hayden's lap, her cheek resting against his chest, their legs intertwined. Her heart thumped hard and she could feel Hayden's matching beat under her ear, and knew it was only partly due to the chance of being caught. Their current position was 95-percent responsible.

Angelica's footsteps arrived at her office door, barely four feet from where they were hidden, with only a partition between them. She flicked the light switch and brightness streamed out, but it was still fairly dark under the desk. Hayden's fingers stroked along her arm, and even through the fabric the caress gave her goose bumps. She glanced up and found him looking languorously down at her, a devilish gleam in his eyes. She shivered.

"I want you," he silently mouthed.

"You're crazy," she mouthed back. His grin showed he was pleased with that pronouncement, and he undid her top button. She wasn't sure whether to laugh or melt. Then when his mouth covered hers, she didn't have to think at all. His hand inched inside her shirt just seconds before he froze, his mouth now a hairsbreadth from hers.

Another set of footsteps was coming down the corridor.

As they heard the footsteps turn in to Angelica's office, Hayden's hand moved away from Lucy's skin, and he redid her top button. "Later," he murmured in her ear.

She bit down on her lip. Later seemed an eternity away.

"Thank you for coming down," Angelica said. With the door open, the words were as clear as if Lucy and Hayden were standing right beside her. Hayden pulled his phone from his pocket and thumbed a button that she assumed started a recording program.

"What the hell couldn't wait for tomorrow morning?"

Lucy jerked as she recognized Graham's voice, but Hayden held her close against his chest, keeping her immobile. Meeting Angelica in the middle of the night didn't look good, but Graham worked crazy hours. There would be an innocent explanation.

"Something I've wanted to tell you for a long time," Angelica said, clearly relishing the words.

"Well, spit it out. I don't have all night." Lucy could imagine Graham checking his watch as he spoke.

"No?" Angelica asked, her voice silky smooth. "Not even for your daughter?"

"What the hell—" Silence filled the air as strongly as the voices had. "Are you telling me…?"

Hayden tipped Lucy's chin up, a question in his eyes, but she shrugged tight shoulders. She didn't know any more than he did, but whatever it was, she didn't like the sound of it.

"Mom always said I had your chin." Angelica's voice was casual, as if she was chatting in a café about the color of her nails. "Surely you've noticed that before?"

"Madeline?"

"Madeline," Angelica said, chuckling. "Now there's a blast from the past. I haven't used that name in a long time."

"Five years you've worked here. *Five years* without mentioning a thing. Why didn't you tell me it was you?" Graham demanded.

"And give you the chance to reject me a second time?"

"I did not reject you! I paid child support. I paid your tuition. I made sure you had everything you needed."

Nausea filled Lucy's stomach, threatening to rise. The only thing keeping her together was Hayden's soothing hand stroking her hair. Angelica was Graham's daughter? They were stepsisters? No wonder Angelica had always hated her—Lucy had Graham's love, affection and public acknowledgment.

"Oh, yes, I had everything," Angelica said. "Except for that small matter of a father. Seems you were saving up all that fatherly affection for your precious Lucy."

Hayden held her more firmly against him. A part of her felt sympathy for Angelica—assuming her story was true—but still, she desperately wanted to run into that office and save Graham from the poison inside his so-called daughter. No matter what he'd done, Graham was worth a hundred Angelicas.

"This has nothing to do with Lucy," Graham growled.

"You're right," Angelica said brightly. "It's all about you. In fact, you're the whole reason I'm here at ANS."

"What are you talking about? Of course you're here because of me—I headhunted you from NCN."

"I've heard you're having some trouble with the congressional hearings. You know, I don't think arresting Brandon Ames and Troy Hall is enough to appease them. They're after the mastermind."

There was a beat of silence, then Graham's voice was incredulous. "It was you."

Angelica chuckled again. "There's no evidence for that theory."

"You manipulated Ames and Hall. Brought out the worst in them."

"I think you have me confused with someone else. But whoever it was wouldn't have had any trouble bringing out the worst in those two sniveling hacks."

"And Marnie? You're the one who brought her in, as well."

"I wouldn't be surprised if she was involved," Angelica said, her tone clearly saying she knew Marnie was. "She's so desperate to make her mark. To shoot to the top."

"And you manipulated that to get her to bring the scheme to me for my approval."

"Not me. She must have done that all on her own."

Graham let out a sigh that sounded as if it came from the bottom of his soul. "Look, I don't want to talk about all that rubbish. Not when I've just found you again."

"And you were so obviously desperate to find me," Angelica said, her voice dripping with sarcasm.

"Maybe not at first. When your mother told me she was pregnant, it threw me. I wasn't expecting that."

"And then there were sixteen years of you still being *thrown?*"

"I'm sorry," he said gruffly. "But at least I'm not like our jerk of a president, who completely abandoned his baby, pretending she didn't exist. I paid child support. Paid for everything you needed."

"Paid?" Her voice turned malicious. "Oh, you're paying, all right. Good luck with that."

"Angelica—" Graham said, clearly confused, but he was cut off.

"Goodbye, Daddy dear." The staccato *tap-tap* of Angelica's heels sounded as she headed down the hallway.

Lucy flung herself from Hayden's arms, out from under the desk, around the partition and into Angelica's office, where Graham was standing as if struck by lightning. He looked up and his face drained of its last remnants of color. She stopped a few feet from him, not sure what to say now that she was here. They stood in silence, not even the sounds of other workers to disguise the emptiness that now stretched between them.

Finally Graham slumped back to sit on Angelica's desk. "So you heard."

"I heard," she said softly, everything inside her breaking apart.

"Lucy, I'm sorry. Of everyone who's been hurt or will be hurt through this mess, I'm most sorry about you." He looked down at his shoes. "I love you more than anyone on earth."

Part of her wanted to hug him and tell him it would be okay, but she'd be lying. And she couldn't make her feet take those last few steps to his side. "You knew," she said. "All this time I've been defending you, *believing* in you, and you've been authorizing Angelica's corrupt scheme."

He recoiled from the accusation, but didn't meet her eyes. "I don't know what to say."

"How about you start by saying you're sorry to Ariella Winthrop for letting her find out about her father's identity live on national television?"

He waved a wrist in the air. "That was an unfortunate side effect."

Her stomach dipped as she realized how little remorse he had. "Was it unfortunate that Ted Morrow had his name dragged through the mud, too?"

"No," he said, his jaw jutting.

She'd heard him rant about the president before, about everything from his policies, to his speeches, to how arrogant he'd been back when they went to school together, but she'd never paid much attention. This time she took him seriously, wanted to understand. "You hate him that much?"

"The truth of the matter is," he said, looking out the dark window, "I've been in love twice in my life. Once was your mother. The other was Darla Sanders, back in college. I thought she loved me, too, that we had a future, but one look from Ted Morrow and she left me without a backward glance. The bastard didn't even marry her."

She opened her mouth and closed it again, unable to believe what she'd heard. "All this has been over a thirty-year-old grudge?"

"Most of it was about good news broadcasting," he said, sounding more like his old self. "People have a right to know about the man who acts on their behalf as their president."

She planted her hands on her hips. "People also have a right to expect that their laws will be followed, no matter whose privacy is involved."

One side of his mouth hitched up. "You're your mother's daughter, Lucy. I'm proud of that."

The warm glow she would normally have felt at such a comment couldn't break through the tumult of other emotions filling her body to the bursting point. She rubbed her temples, trying to keep herself from falling into pieces on the floor of Angelica's office. There would be time enough for falling apart later, after she had some answers.

"And Angelica?" she asked. "Whose daughter is she?"

He heaved out a sigh. "She was raised by her mother, but it seems she's ended up with my ruthlessness anyway."

Hayden stepped into the room and all the breath left

Lucy's body. She'd forgotten he was outside the door, listening to everything she and Graham said. She ran the conversation back through her mind, praying she hadn't led Graham deeper into trouble.

"What the hell is he doing here?" Graham boomed.

Hayden drove his hands in his pockets, a picture of immovability. "I came with Lucy."

Graham turned to Lucy, his jaw slack. "You brought him here?"

She looked up at Hayden, unsure how much she was allowed to divulge. He gave her a resigned shrug, followed by a nod. She opened her mouth, but now that she had permission, she didn't know what to say. Couldn't think of how to explain. Hayden nodded again, encouraging her.

She turned back to her stepfather. "Hayden suspected you and Angelica were involved in the illegal hackings. I assured him you weren't and I was helping him so I could clear your name."

"By eavesdropping on me?" Graham asked, looking from one to the other, outraged.

Unused to being the target of her stepfather's displeasure, Lucy flinched. Then she collected herself. He might have dug his own grave—she had no illusions now about that—but this would still be hard on him. And it was only going to get worse. She could be tolerant of his emotional reactions under stress—he'd certainly cut her some slack during her attempts at rebellion as a teenager.

"Graham," she said gently, "we had no idea you'd be in Angelica's office."

Understanding dawned in his eyes. "You were after her."

Hayden nodded. "This time, yes."

"I guess you heard the conversation, too?" It was a

question, but Graham already seemed resigned to the inevitability of the answer.

"I did," Hayden said, his face neutral.

Graham narrowed his eyes. "Did you get enough on us?"

"On you, yes. Angelica didn't actually admit to anything." Hayden picked up a glass paperweight from Angelica's desk, looked it over and replaced it, timing the pause it created like the pro he was. "You know, it would help your case if you cooperated about her role in the hacking."

Graham groaned, then covered his eyes with a thick hand. "I can't do that. She was right—I've failed her in almost every way a father could." He dropped his hand and met Hayden's gaze steadily. "The only thing I can do for her now is protect her in this."

"It won't be enough to save her," Hayden warned.

"We'll see." Graham let out a slow lungful of air. "So what happens now?"

"You, Marnie and Angelica will be called to testify before the congressional committee. They'll have my notes, so they'll be able to ask the right questions."

"I'll make you a deal, Black," he said gruffly. "I'll confess to everything I've done if you'll keep Angelica's—and Madeline's—name out of it."

Hayden rocked back on his heels as he considered, then nodded and thrust his hands back into his pockets. "I don't have the authority to make that deal, but I'll take it to the people who do, and see what they say."

"I appreciate it." Graham scrubbed the pads of his fingers over his face and Lucy could almost see him growing smaller. "What's next after I testify?"

Hayden didn't blink. "There will likely be a jail term, and you'll have to sell ANS. The regulators won't allow you to keep ownership of a broadcast network once you plead guilty to the crimes you've committed."

"No," Lucy said, refusing to consider jail as an option.

"Lucy." Graham sounded heartbreakingly weary. "Sweetheart, it might be unavoidable once I testify."

"No," she said again and turned to Hayden. "If a deal can be made to protect Angelica, then a deal can be made to protect Graham."

"It's not the same thing," Hayden said. "There's nothing to bargain with for Graham's freedom. What would you have me do?"

"I don't know—as you've said several times, this is your area of specialty." She reached for Hayden's hands and interlaced their fingers, bringing them to rest over her heart. "You can save him. He's the only family I have. Please don't take him."

"Lucy, I'm sorry," he said, his voice strained. "There's nothing I can do."

Damn him, he even had the gall to look torn, despite this being the outcome he'd wanted from the beginning— he'd always wanted Graham's conviction more than any other. *Of course* he wouldn't help simply because the woman he'd been having a fling with asked him to.

She dropped his hands, straightened her spine and focused on the most important thing. "Can he at least go home?"

Hayden cleared his throat. "Yes, but he'll be called to appear before the congressional-committee hearing, probably in a couple of days." He turned to Graham, expression stern. "You won't leave town, will you?"

"Of course he won't," Lucy snapped, moving beside her stepfather as he sat on the desk, providing a united front. "Come on, Graham. I'm taking you home."

Graham's shoulders were rounded with defeat and when

he looked up at her, his eyes were as bleak as a winter's night. "Rosie's up in my office."

"Hayden, can I trust that you'll see yourself out of the building without stopping anywhere you shouldn't?" Her voice had an edge of contempt that she hadn't intended, but it was there anyway.

A confused line appeared on Hayden's forehead. "Sure."

"Then I'll say goodbye." She said the words quickly— like ripping a bandage off, it would surely hurt less if it happened fast. "We won't be running our exposé now, so you're in the clear. And you finally have the head you wanted on a platter. I guess we're finished with what we've been working on together."

He looked at her for a long moment. "I guess we are," he said and turned on his heel. She watched him walk to the elevator from Angelica's office door—he didn't glance backward once.

With every step he took, something deep inside her pulled, as if it were attached to him and was being stretched to breaking point. Their rules had made it clear that what they had would only last so long. Both of them had wanted it that way. Catching Graham meant their time was up. But when Hayden stepped inside the elevator, whatever had been inside her was now gone, leaving her empty. Hollow. Gouged out.

She closed her eyes against the emotion stinging them and turned back to Graham. She had a job to do—Graham needed her. She linked her elbow in his and pulled him to his feet. "Let's go get Rosebud and go home."

"Lucy," he said, letting her see emotion in his eyes without shying away from it for the first time since she'd known him. "I really am sorry."

"I know, Graham. It's okay." But her heart was dying inside. The only two people she loved in the world were going to leave her. One for—in all probability—jail, and the other for his life in New York.

She'd just lied to Graham, because nothing was okay. And she couldn't see things being okay again.

Eleven

Sitting on a kitchen stool in her pajamas as the sun peeked over the horizon, Lucy watched the early morning news, a steaming mug of coffee between her hands. It was blanket coverage of Graham's testimony yesterday at the congressional committee's hearing. She pointed the remote at the TV and flicked to NCN, where they were replaying yesterday's footage of Graham being taken into custody. He'd also been ordered by the Federal Communications Commission to sell ANS, or else the network would lose its license. What they didn't know yet was that Liam Crowe, a self-made media mogul, had already made an offer to buy ANS—that would be announced later today.

They were also reporting that Marnie Salloway would be testifying in a few hours, since Graham's testimony had been that she'd been the one who'd kept him in the loop about the hacking and brought new developments to him to get approval. She was expected to be charged by week's end. As Lucy had expected, Graham hadn't mentioned Angelica once, and hadn't been questioned about her. The prosecutors and congressional committee had taken the deal Graham had offered, including keeping his relationship with Angelica private, which meant the media hadn't picked up on the story...yet.

Lucy blinked away tears for Graham. She'd stayed with him the night she and Hayden had overheard his conversation with Angelica, the night her life had fallen apart. She'd taken him to his place and slept in a spare room. Or pretended to sleep—she'd barely had more than an hour's sleep at a time since then. He'd been taken into custody yesterday afternoon and she'd brought Rosie back here. She'd fallen asleep for just over an hour at about three in the morning, and now she was wide-awake again.

She couldn't stop thinking about Graham's miserable future, about his involvement in the illegal phone hacking, about him being Angelica's father. It was almost too much to comprehend, as if everything she'd ever believed was wrong.

And when she hadn't been thinking about Graham, her mind stubbornly turned to the one subject she'd been fighting to avoid.

Hayden.

Her eyes drifted closed and she saw his face, his smoldering coffee-brown eyes, his darkened jaw needing a shave at the end of the day. Her chest ripped open, painfully exposing her vulnerable heart. She had no idea how long she'd been denying it, but it was clear now—she loved him. And she'd never been more miserable in her life. Wasn't love supposed to be uplifting?

All her original reservations about getting involved with an older man and undoing her work to make something of her life were still there, but they'd been dwarfed by what had happened in the past week. The thing was, her love for Hayden was now tainted. It would always be smeared by Graham's arrest—she'd never be able to think about Hayden again without it being tangled up with the heartache of what had become of her stepfather.

What had he said to her that night in Montana?

"If we let it linger, it'll turn into something neither of us wanted. Something that might become bitter, and I don't want anything to tarnish the memories I'm taking of you."

It had happened anyway, even without them letting it linger. Now she was left without the sweet memories of her time with Hayden to keep her warm at night. They'd been ruined.

The best she could hope for was a little more time with him before he caught Angelica, finished the investigation…and left. He might not want to see her again after she'd been so rude the other night, and it wouldn't be the same now, but if wanting whatever she could have from him made her desperate, then she was willing to cop to the charge. She'd call him today. Maybe they could make some new rules. Or maybe she was deluding herself and everything was too tainted for even their fling to survive anymore.

Her cell rang, and she reached across the counter to retrieve it from where she'd thrown it last night. She wasn't in the mood to talk to most people, but she needed to keep an eye out for calls from Graham or the facility he'd been taken to.

When she picked it up, her heart stuttered. The number on the screen was Hayden's.

"Did I wake you?" The voice, so deep and familiar, made her ache.

"No," she said, her voice raspy. "I've been awake for a while."

"Can I talk to you?"

"You are talking to me."

"In person."

She squeezed her eyes shut. At this time of the morning, she didn't have her head together enough to face anyone, let alone Hayden Black, with all the conflicting emotions he stirred within her. She wanted to talk to him when she was ready, when her head was clear. Perhaps after another coffee—or three. "I can meet you in a couple of hours."

"I'm on the street in front of your place."

Her heart thudded against her ribs as she slipped off the stool and padded through to the front window. As she drew the drapes aside, she saw Hayden's rental car on the street. "So you are."

"Can I come in for a few minutes?"

"It's not a great time, Hayden." She needed a chance to talk to him about resurrecting their fling for as long as she could have him. And the time to convince him wasn't early in the morning while she was in her pajamas and had only consumed one cup of coffee.

"It has to be now," he said, and something in his voice reached out and pulled at her.

"Sure," she said on a sigh, knowing she'd probably regret it. It was hard to be seductive in striped pajamas after an hour's sleep. She disconnected and threw the cell on a side table. She didn't have time to change, but she ducked into her bedroom and grabbed her royal-blue satin dressing gown.

She swung the door open to find him standing there with a sleepy Josh in one arm. She stared at Hayden in his dark trousers, pale blue shirt and tie and dark suit jacket, her belly tightening. All she wanted to do was take those clothes off him.

"Sorry it's so early," he said, his thoughts clearly not on the same track as hers.

"Come on in." She leaned over to kiss Josh on the cheek, trying not to linger and sink into the scent of Hayden, then turned and walked down the hall to the kitchen. "Do you want a coffee?"

"No, thanks," he said, bending to scratch Rosie behind the ears, then depositing a rapidly waking Josh on the floor beside her. "I won't be here long."

She poured another coffee for herself anyway and took a sip. Any assistance to her mental alertness was welcome. "So this visit is both early and quick."

"I came to say goodbye," he said, his voice deep yet devoid of emotion.

Her stomach fell fast. She carefully placed the mug on the counter before she dropped it. He was leaving? It was too soon. Too soon. She held on to the edges of the counter for support.

"Hayden," she said, then swallowed. "I'm sorry about what I said the other night. I was upset."

His features seemed carefully schooled to give nothing away. "It wasn't anything you said, Lucy. I need to go."

"Before the investigation is finished?"

"It's for the best. I've become too involved. One of the top investigators in my company, John Harris, will be here by tonight. He'll be more impartial, which is what the investigation needs now." He frowned and looked down at Josh, who was petting Rosie. "What it always needed."

"And you're leaving D.C.?" She'd known this moment was coming, of course she had, but *please* not yet. She wasn't ready.

He nodded and a muscle jumped in his jaw. "The flight to New York is in a couple of hours. Our bags are packed."

She sucked in a breath and ignored the ache in her chest. There was no chance of a future for them—and if she'd had any doubts about that, he'd settled them at her aunt's lodge in Montana—so maybe he was right to leave now. Only ten minutes ago she'd been thinking that things between them were probably too tainted to survive even their fling with all its rules. Perhaps they'd even make things worse if they didn't make a clean break now. Wanting a little more time with him was simply the desperate need of a woman in love who was in denial about the future she couldn't have.

She lifted her chin and found a polite smile, determined to see him off with at least that civility. "Thank you for dropping by to say goodbye."

He speared his fingers through his hair and held them there, gripping tight for a long moment before dropping his hands to his sides. "Damn it, I hate this formality between us."

"We can't have it both ways, Hayden. This was only ever temporary." A blanket of calm descended to smother the tumultuous emotions that had been battering her. Acceptance. It wouldn't last long, she knew, but she was grateful for its appearance now. "Thanks for organizing Graham's deal to keep Angelica's name out of the hearings. I want to see justice catch up with her, but I know Graham would have hated himself if it had come via him."

Hayden nodded but seemed distracted. "It was a good deal for us—he gave a full and frank confession, and he named names like Marnie Salloway. We'll catch Angelica. The deal was only to keep her name out of Graham's interview. Now that that's over, all bets are off."

"But it won't be you who catches her," she said softly.

"No." He lifted his broad shoulders in a shrug. "John Harris will work the case. But I'll keep an eye on it from the New York office."

The casual way he was talking about leaving grated on her nerves. "So you're walking away."

"I'm taking my son home," he said pointedly. "It's the right thing to do."

"Is it so easy to leave me?" As soon as she said the words, she wanted to snatch them back. Pointlessly, she covered her mouth with two fingers, as if that could help. Where had that acceptance gone?

His eyes flashed fire. "Hell, this isn't even close to easy, Lucy. But yes, I'm leaving." He held one palm out, as if in surrender. "I can't give you what you need."

The words were like a match to tinder—all those turbulent emotions that had been roiling inside her finally had a reason to coalesce. "Who are you to tell me what I need?" she demanded.

"I'll tell you what I know," he said in measured tones. "I'm cynical and world-weary. A jaded widower. I know I'll never love with an open and unguarded heart, or with the intensity that I once did. My heart simply isn't capable of it—it's like an old, beaten-up, secondhand car. You deserve someone full of life. Optimism. Verve. Like you."

An ironic laugh bubbled up from deep down, but died before it reached her lips. He was telling her what she needed again. And he'd never been more wrong. Suddenly she saw everything clearly, maybe for the first time. Her love wasn't tainted—it just had some obstacles to overcome. But love took two. Unrequited love was a totally different ball game, and it seemed that was the only type he was offering.

"You're wrong," she said, staring him down. "But if

you're not even willing to stand by me and believe in what we could have, then maybe it is better that you go now."

He rubbed a hand over his eyes. "I've made a mess of this from the start."

"I fell in love with you, you know." She spoke the words lightly, more of an observation than recrimination. It was fair that he knew.

His face drained of color as if she'd slapped him. "God, I'm sorry, Lucy. So sorry."

Sorry? Her bottom lip trembled. If he said that word a third time she didn't know if she could bear it. "It's not your fault," she said more sharply than she intended. "It's mine."

His gaze stayed fixed on her face, obviously not fooled for a moment. "One more reason I need to leave. Once I'm gone I won't be able to hurt you anymore."

Inside her everything screamed, *just stay! Stay with me.* But she refused to beg. If there had been a moment for him to declare he wanted to be with her, it was when she'd told him she loved him. He'd simply apologized.

She wouldn't let the stinging at the back of her eyes turn into tears. All she had left was her dignity, and she was hanging on to that with everything inside her. She crossed to the sink and tipped the cold coffee out, then turned to face him, tranquil mask in place.

"So this is it," she said, crossing her arms under her breasts.

"Yes." He drummed the fingers of one hand on the side of his thigh. "I expect I'll be seeing you on the TV. Probably as a news anchor, but realistically, as anything you want. You have talent, Lucy."

After seeing what had become of Angelica, Marnie and Graham in the pursuit of ratings, the thought made her sick. "I don't think my future is in broadcast journalism. I'll be tendering my resignation to the new owner of ANS today."

His gaze sharpened. "What will you do instead?"

"I don't know. I think I'll take a couple of months off and find out what I'd like to do with my life." She was in no place right now to make life-changing decisions.

"Whatever you do, I know you'll make a success of it." The kind words, gently spoken, were almost harder to take than if he'd dismissed her plans. She pulled the sash of her robe tighter and held on to her composure by the most tenuous of threads.

"And you'll do a great job with Josh," she said truthfully. "He's a lucky boy to have you as a father." She was going to miss Josh like crazy. The little boy had wormed his way into her heart and even if she never saw him again, he'd always have a place there.

He nodded, then cleared his throat. "We need to go so we can make that flight."

He stepped toward her and she turned away, unable to stand seeing him that near and not have him. "Lucy," he whispered as he cupped the side of her face with his palm, then, without warning, he pulled her against him with his other hand and kissed her fiercely. The last shred of her control evaporated and she kissed him back just as hungrily. His fingers dug into her upper arms, and she welcomed the sensation, wanting to feel everything that was left for them. Lacing her fingers at the nape of his neck, she pulled down, never wanting to let him go, wishing the moment could last forever, holding him as tightly as she could. She felt her tears sliding down her cheeks and mingling with their kiss but was helpless to stop them. When his hand gripped her knee and urged it up, she wrapped a leg around his waist, desperate with the need to be closer.

Too soon, he wrenched his mouth away and rested his

forehead on hers, panting. Then, without a word, he placed a brief kiss on her forehead, picked up a smiling Josh and walked down the hall. Eyes squeezed shut, she listened to his footsteps fading as they got farther away, until her front door opened and closed. Only then did she slide down the cupboards to the floor and let the tears fall unrestrained.

Twelve

Holding the fracturing parts of herself together by sheer force of will a couple of hours later, Lucy walked through the heavy door a guard held open for her into a cold and drab pale green room. Graham was already waiting for her, seeming much smaller—shorter, even—with his shoulders hunched down, his lack of expansive movements. Unlike his usual warm greeting, his eyes were studiously locked on his hands, tightly clasped on the table.

Perhaps it was her own perceptions, as well. Graham had always been such a larger-than-life character to her— her stepfather since she was twelve, the owner of a national news network, a man confident of his place in the world. Now incarcerated while he awaited his court date to enter his guilty plea and receive his sentence, he was wearing an orange jumpsuit, stripped of all the trappings of his position and wealth. He hadn't even been granted the option of posting bail—with the seriousness of the charges against him, his private wealth and no real family to hold him, he'd been assessed a flight risk.

As she slid into the brown plastic chair, Graham looked up for the first time and the uncertainty there, the fear of rejection, made her heart weep. It hadn't occurred to her that he'd doubt her love and steadfastness.

"You're a sweet girl for coming," he said in a thick voice.

"Sweetness has nothing to do with it. You're my step-father and I love you."

His jaw worked hard before he spoke. "Even after everything?"

"No matter what," she said quietly. "You've always been there for me and now I'm here for you."

He covered his face for long moments and when he dropped his hands, his eyes were misty. "I'm sorry, Lucy."

Seemed today was her day to receive apologies from the men in her life. "I can't say that I'm okay with what you've done at ANS," she said, "but that's only one part of who you are. You're also the man who took me into your heart when you married my mother, and kept me there even after she was gone. You're the man who wanted the best for me, gave me a job and kept me out of the dirty goings-on at ANS."

"That was always my stipulation—nothing was to touch you," he said fiercely. "Those involved were never to draw you into it."

That was Graham all over—he had honor, he just drew different lines about where it began and ended the than rest of the world. But she never doubted he'd prioritize her and protect her. Which would have gone down well with Angelica, she thought with a wry smile. It would have fed her hatred—not only was Graham like a father to Lucy, but he'd protected her while allowing Angelica to dive into illegal work.

"How's Rosebud?" he asked.

Rosie had whined overnight when she'd realized she wasn't going home to Graham, so Lucy had let her get under the covers with her. "Missing you, but I've been keeping her busy, so I think she's fairly happy."

"Thank you for taking her in."

"Having her has been good for me, too." A warm body to cuddle on the sofa this morning when the world looked dark had been priceless. She'd lost Hayden, the man she loved; Josh, the little boy she yearned for; and her stepfather, all in one fell swoop. Rosie had lost her human— her only family—so they'd been consoling each other.

"Lucy," Graham said carefully. "There's something between you and Black, isn't there?"

A denial was on the tip of her tongue, but why hide now? Hayden was gone, someone else from his company would be here soon to take over the rest of the investigation and the worst had already happened for Graham. There was no reason left to keep the secret.

She swallowed to get her voice to work. "There was for me, yes."

"Do you love him?" he asked sharply.

Suddenly there wasn't enough air in the little room. "It's not that simple. There are—"

"It *is* that simple," he said, cutting her off. "Do you love him?"

"Yes," she whispered.

"Let me tell you something. When I look back over my life, there are things I wish I had done differently. But my chief regret is about your mother."

She blinked. "I thought you loved her?"

"I did. A great deal. More than she knew. I should have

told her more. Cherished her more. She was the love of my life, but I spent my time building empires. I thought we had forever, but we only had seven years together. Too short. Much too short. She's gone, and ANS is gone now, too, so all that time I sacrificed from my marriage for ANS was for nothing."

"She knew you loved her," Lucy said truthfully. "She knew."

"Thanks." A small, nostalgic smile brushed over his mouth before he pinned her with his gaze. "Now it's your turn."

There seemed to be advice in his words, but it didn't make sense. "Don't you hate Hayden? He's the one who pursued you until you ended up here."

"If I never lay eyes on that man again it will be too soon," he said heatedly. "But much as I might hate him, I love you more. I'd give anything to make you happy, sweetheart."

"Thank you," she said past the tightness in her throat.

He looked directly into her eyes, not bothering to hide his emotions as he usually did. "If this is love, Lucy, grab it. Treasure it. Don't let anything stand in your way."

"What if he doesn't want to grab it back? If—" The pain of his apology in response to telling him she loved him took hold, until she was able to stuff it back down and take a breath. "If he's walked away?"

"Then he's an idiot, just as I suspected." He leaned forward in his chair. "But if you still love him, go get what you want. Life's too short, too unpredictable to waste a second of it."

Lucy looked hard at the man sitting across from her. This wasn't the same man she'd known—she'd always been a bit in awe of that man, who'd been a little distant, despite their closeness. He'd never talked to her about his relationship with her mother, never opened himself this way. Even though her world was crumbling around her, and she'd do almost anything to save Graham from being incarcerated, this—their first ever heart-to-heart—was like a small ray of sunshine shining through the parted clouds.

"He has a son," she found herself saying. "Hayden Black. He's a widower with a one-year-old son called Josh."

Graham's face folded up into a frown. "You're too young to become a mother."

Not long ago, she would have thought the same. Since becoming part of Josh's life, though, she saw motherhood and parenting differently, as something she'd relish if she had the opportunity. She'd been involved with babies through her charity for years, but getting to know Josh had been a new experience. And, no question, she'd fallen head over heels in love with the little boy.

"He's such a special boy. And he loves Rosie," she said, remembering how cute they were together. "The first time I met him, I had Rosie with me and he called out 'Goggie.' When I met him again the next day, he wanted to know where she was."

"You haven't asked me about Angelica," Graham said abruptly.

She hesitated, trying to catch the change of direction the conversation had suddenly taken. "That's your business. I won't pry."

"I never should have abandoned her as a baby." He clenched a fist on the table. "I thought I was doing enough by paying money to keep a roof over her head and food in her belly. Sending her to school. But it *wasn't* enough. I should have seen that at the time instead of being focused on my own distaste about being weighed down by a baby…or her annoying mother. If I'd raised Madeline, maybe things would have been different." His expression drooped, as if the weight of the world was on his shoulders. "Maybe she wouldn't have turned out so bitter."

She bit down on her bottom lip. Maybe Angelica would have been different had Graham raised her—he certainly should have tried. Though saying that wouldn't be helpful to a man already riddled with regrets, and in all honesty, was that the only problem Angelica had? She couldn't think of a single useful thing to say, so she went with the generic. "Babies are so precious."

"You obviously have feelings for Josh," Graham said, pointing a finger at her. "So you're poised to repeat both of my biggest mistakes in one giant blunder. Are you ready to walk away from the man you love, as well as a kid you want to be yours?"

She leaned back in her chair, folding her arms under her breasts as if she could pull herself away from the terrible picture he painted. "I don't know, but I promise I'll think about it."

He nodded, satisfied. "I know you'll do the right thing. You always do." He pushed his chair back and stood. "Now you go on and leave me here. You don't want to spend your days keeping an old man company."

"I'll be back to see you again before your court appearance," she said, keeping the tears that threatened in check. The last thing Graham needed was to think he'd made her cry. "Whatever happens with your sentencing, I'll be here for you."

By the time she made it to her car, she couldn't hold the tears back any longer. She rested her head on the steering wheel and let them come. Tears for Graham mingled with tears for herself as they slid down her cheeks.

If you still love him, go get what you want. Life's too short, too unpredictable to waste a second of it.

This time his words struck a chord deep inside her. Graham was right. She loved Hayden. It was as simple—and as gloriously complicated—as that.

She didn't care if Hayden had some ridiculous idea about their suitability or his heart's capabilities. She was going to fight for their love, fight for them. All the other reasons they'd thought they shouldn't be together, they were molehills, not mountains. Anything could be surmounted if they did it hand in hand. If she'd learned one thing from Graham's example, it was not to live with regrets. To make changes in her life while she could. Even if talking to Hayden again was destined to fail, she at least had to try.

She checked her watch—still early enough to catch a flight. She reached for her cell, dialed her travel agent and bought a round-trip ticket to New York. She'd just have enough time to get home, grab a couple of things and make the flight. She couldn't take Rosie, so she'd need to be back in D.C. tonight. If things worked out with Hayden, Rosie would be part of their permanent plans, but for today, she'd have to wait here. Excitement fluttered in her stomach. She knew what she wanted and she was going to grab it.

When a light turned red, she drummed her fingers on the steering wheel. First order of business—she needed to work out what to say when she saw Hayden again. He'd been adamant this morning, so she'd need the perfect way to explain that nothing mattered more than the two of them creating a new family with Josh and their future children. Words swirled around her head, forming into sentences to convince him, then fell apart as she discarded them. Maybe on the plane—she'd have a bit of time on the plane to get the words just perfect. She should be thinking about what to grab at her house so that went as quickly as possible. Missing this flight was not an option.

She pulled up in front of her place, grabbed her hold-all bag and flung open the car door. As she stepped out onto the road, she hesitated. Someone was sitting on the concrete steps to her front door. Two someones. Her heart stilled. Two someones she loved. Hayden stood and picked up Josh, but he didn't make a move to come over to her.

Her knees wobbled and she leaned against the car for support. His gaze met hers but it gave nothing away. He'd come back—did he need something, maybe some more testimony? Had he left something in her house? Clothes? His phone?

The plan had been to tell him what she wanted for their future, but that was supposed to happen *after* she'd had time to get it straight in her head. Make the words perfect so she didn't ruin the chance. But he was here. Earlier than her plan. She was going to have to make the best of it.

She put her handbag up on her shoulder and set the keyless lock. Then she took a deep breath and pushed away from the car. One foot in front of the other. As she approached, Josh squealed and reached for her, but Hayden kept his hold on him.

"Hello," Hayden said, a slight frown line marring his brow.

She straightened her spine and found a welcoming smile. "Did you forget something?"

"Yes."

Her heart shattered and she only held herself upright through sheer force of will. He'd returned because he'd forgotten something. Though that didn't mean she couldn't convince him. "You'd better come in."

She moved around him and unlocked her front door. If she could get them inside, she'd have a better chance of having a fair hearing for what she needed to say. Maybe lock the door behind them. She pushed the door open with a trembling hand. Rosie rushed at them and greeted everyone with the enthusiasm of a dog who hadn't seen people for hours, standing on her hind legs and wagging her curly tail.

Forming her argument in her mind, Lucy walked into her living room. It was a safe place for Josh to crawl around on the floor so she could have all of Hayden's attention. Then she swiveled and planted her hands on her hips. "Before you get whatever it is you forgot, there's something I—"

"You," he said, voice deep and serious.

She stopped midsentence, mouth still open to form the next word. "Pardon?"

He put Josh on the sofa, where he was immediately joined by Rosie. Then Hayden looked back to Lucy, eyes intense. "I forgot *you*. As soon as the plane took off, I knew I'd made a stupid mistake. A colossal mistake. When we disembarked in New York, I found a flight straight back again."

She started to tremble. The hope was so strong, it was painful, but none of this made sense. "You want to continue our fling?" she asked.

"I want more than a damn fling. I want *everything*, Lucy." He took her hands and gripped them tightly. "I want to live my life with you."

The trembling inside grew stronger, until she could feel her lips quivering, and her fingers as Hayden's gripped them. All that she wanted seemed *so* close, but she wouldn't live with regrets. She wouldn't settle for anything less than the whole package.

"What about Josh?" she asked, looking down at the little boy who was rubbing Rosie's tummy. "I couldn't be with you and be excluded from your relationship with him. You said you'd never share him again."

"I was wrong." He dropped her hands and speared his fingers through his hair, looking nervous. "One of the things I thought about on that flight was that parenting a child with you would be a world apart from parenting with Brooke. It was fear talking—fear of being edged out of my son's life again. The best thing for Josh is to have two parents who love him. But I know it's asking a lot to take on me and Josh together. You should be—"

She placed a finger over his lips. "You're not about to tell me what I should be doing again, are you?"

His mouth curved under her fingers. "No, ma'am."

"Good," she said and grinned. "Because I love Josh. When you flew away, I was missing him almost as much as I was missing you. I want you both as a package deal."

His Adam's apple bobbed slowly, then he knelt down on her living room carpet and took her hands. "Lucy Royall, marry me. Marry me and Josh."

Joy bubbled through her body, filling every cell, every dark corner inside her until it was too big to be contained and seemed to flow out and fill even the air around her. But, aside from a smile, she managed to keep from reacting just yet.

"Before I answer that," she said sweetly, laying her Southern accent on thick, "I want to set some ground rules."

His mouth opened. Closed again. "Ground rules? You're killing me, Lucy."

She held up a finger. "First rule—no more thinking you know what's best for me."

"Agreed," he said, chuckling. "I failed pretty bad at that anyway."

"Also, I'll be flying back to D.C. at least once a week to

visit Graham no matter what happens with his sentencing, so I don't want to live too far away. Though I won't want to be far away after he gets out, either." She'd meant it when she'd told Graham earlier that she'd be there for him.

Not letting go of her hands, Hayden stood. "I expected you'd want to be nearby and I've had a suggestion. I'm open to setting up an office for my business in D.C. if you want to stay here. Or we could live in both cities—Josh has a few years before he starts school, so we don't have to be chained anywhere just yet. We'll work around Boyle's sentence."

After tracking Graham's crimes and being the one responsible for catching him, Hayden was still willing to work around the man's sentence, to change his business, if needed? For her. Because he knew it was important to her. In that moment, she knew he genuinely loved her. "You'd really be happy with that?"

"I learned a couple of things from my first marriage. This time I want a true partnership, where our lives reflect what we both want, what we both need. Graham is part of your life, so we'll include him. I'm sure I'll come to appreciate his virtues," he said wryly. "One thing I do like about him is he honestly cares for you. I can respect that."

Emotion clogging her throat, she wrapped her arms around his waist. "I didn't think I could love you more." It was almost too much, and tears of joy began to creep down her cheeks. "You know, he told me about an hour ago that I should come after you. I've booked a flight to New York. I was going to convince you to give us a chance."

He chuckled. "Who would have thought I had Boyle to thank for something good?" He tucked her head against his chest, smoothing her hair down. "Your house is too big for one person anyway—we may as well fill it up. Why do you have such a big place?"

"Build it and they will come," she quoted softly. Being an only child who'd lost both her parents, she hadn't been able to contemplate a condo or something small. "I think I've always been waiting for a family of my own."

"You have one now." His voice was as rough as gravel. "Josh, me and Rosebud."

Rosebud came trotting over at the sound of her name, panting with her curly tongue peeking out. Lucy looked from Rosie to Josh on the sofa to Hayden in her arms. And smiled. "The perfect family."

"So is that the end of your ground rules?" Hayden asked, leaning back enough so she could see his eyes.

"Yes." There was nothing more she could possibly want. She was ready to marry the man she loved. "I'll—"

"Well, I have a couple of my own before you answer my proposal." He pulled her down on the sofa so they were sitting with Josh—Lucy in Hayden's lap and Josh in Lucy's, with Hayden's arms around both.

She blinked. "You do?"

"First ground rule," he said, eyes narrowed, "no more secrecy. If I want to kiss you in the middle of a park, or on the steps of the Capitol, I will."

She bit down on the wide smile that threatened, needing to at least appear serious in the negotiations. "I think I can live with that rule."

Obviously bored with the lack of action, Josh crawled out of Lucy's lap and over to the other end of the sofa and began patting Rosie's nose, giggling when she licked his fingers on each pat.

"Second rule," Hayden said, bringing her attention back to him by maneuvering her to straddle his lap, then resting his hands on her hips. "There are no conditions on where we can make love anymore. Only being able to have you at your place was driving me insane."

She kissed a path across his jaw and was rewarded when he shuddered. "Another rule I can wholeheartedly approve," she murmured in his ear.

"Then—" he cradled her face in his palms, bringing it back in front of his "—I think we might just have ourselves an agreement to get married."

The intensity in his eyes, his love for her that was shining there unguarded, made everything inside her sing. Then he captured her mouth and kissed her, and she knew she'd never want more than this: being with the man she loved, who loved her, and the family of her heart.

* * * * *

REQUEST YOUR FREE BOOKS!

2 FREE NOVELS PLUS 2 FREE GIFTS!

◆HARLEQUIN®

Desire

ALWAYS POWERFUL, PASSIONATE AND PROVOCATIVE

YES! Please send me 2 FREE Harlequin Desire® novels and my 2 FREE gifts (gifts are worth about $10). After receiving them, if I don't wish to receive any more books, I can return the shipping statement marked "cancel." If I don't cancel, I will receive 6 brand-new novels every month and be billed just $4.30 per book in the U.S. or $4.99 per book in Canada. That's a savings of at least 14% off the cover price! It's quite a bargain! Shipping and handling is just 50¢ per book in the U.S. and 75¢ per book in Canada.* I understand that accepting the 2 free books and gifts places me under no obligation to buy anything. I can always return a shipment and cancel at any time. Even if I never buy another book, the two free books and gifts are mine to keep forever.

225/320 HDN FVP7

Name _____ (PLEASE PRINT)

Address _____ Apt. #

City _____ State/Prov. _____ Zip/Postal Code

Signature (if under 18, a parent or guardian must sign)

Mail to the Harlequin® Reader Service:
IN U.S.A.: P.O. Box 1867, Buffalo, NY 14240-1867
IN CANADA: P.O. Box 609, Fort Erie, Ontario L2A 5X3

**Want to try two free books from another line?
Call 1-800-873-8635 or visit www.ReaderService.com.**

* Terms and prices subject to change without notice. Prices do not include applicable taxes. Sales tax applicable in N.Y. Canadian residents will be charged applicable taxes. Offer not valid in Quebec. This offer is limited to one order per household. Not valid for current subscribers to Harlequin Desire books. All orders subject to credit approval. Credit or debit balances in a customer's account(s) may be offset by any other outstanding balance owed by or to the customer. Please allow 4 to 6 weeks for delivery. Offer available while quantities last.

Your Privacy—The Harlequin® Reader Service is committed to protecting your privacy. Our Privacy Policy is available online at www.ReaderService.com or upon request from the Harlequin Reader Service.

We make a portion of our mailing list available to reputable third parties that offer products we believe may interest you. If you prefer that we not exchange your name with third parties, or if you wish to clarify or modify your communication preferences, please visit us at www.ReaderService.com/consumerschoice or write to us at Harlequin Reader Service Preference Service, P.O. Box 9062, Buffalo, NY 14269. Include your complete name and address.

HDI3

Vincenzo Arsenio D'Agostino stared at his king and reached the only logical conclusion.

The man had lost his mind.

Ferruccio Selvaggio-D'Agostino—the bastard king, as his opponents called him—twisted his lips. "Do pick your jaw off the floor, Vincenzo. No, I'm *not* insane. Get. A. Wife. ASAP."

Dio. He'd said it again.

Mockery gleamed in Ferruccio's eyes. "I've needed you on this job for *years,* but that playboy image you've been cultivating is notorious. And that image won't cut it in the leagues I need you to play in now. When you're representing Castaldini, Vincenzo, I want the media to cover only your achievements on behalf of the kingdom."

Vincenzo shook his head in disbelief. "*Dio!* When did you become such a stick in the mud, Ferruccio?"

"If you mean when did I become an advocate for marriage and family life, where have you been the last four years? I'm the living, breathing ad for both. And it's time I did you the favor of shoving you onto that path."

"What path? The one to happily-ever-after? Don't you know that's a mirage most men pursue until they drop in defeat?"

Ferruccio went on, "You're pushing forty…"

"I'm thirty-eight!"

"…*and* you've been alone since your parents died two decades ago…"

"I have friends!"

"…*whom* you don't have time for and who don't have time for you." Ferruccio raised his hand, aborting his interjection. "Make a new family, Vincenzo. It's the best thing you can do for yourself, and incidentally, for the kingdom."

"Next you'll dictate the wife I should 'get.'"

"If you don't decide, I will." Ferruccio gave him his signature discussion-ending smile. "'Get a wife' wasn't a request. It's a royal decree."

But Vincenzo knew it wouldn't be that easy. Like his king, Vincenzo had been a one-woman man. Unlike his king, he'd blown his one-off shot on an illusion.

Even after six years, the memory of her sank its tentacles into his mind, making his muscles feel as if they'd snap….

A realization went off in his head like a solar flare.

A smile tugged at his lips, fueled by what he hadn't felt in six years. Excitement. Anticipation.

All he needed was enough leverage against Glory Monaghan to make his proposal an offer she couldn't refuse.

Will Glory say yes?

Find out in

TEMPORARILY HIS PRINCESS by Olivia Gates.

Available May 2013 from Harlequin® Desire wherever books are sold!

HDEXP0413